Appalachian Witness

Volume 24 - 2021

Pine Mountain Sand & Gravel
Contemporary Appalachian Writing

2021

Pine Mountain Sand &Gravel

Contemporary Appalachian Writing

VOLUME 24 : 2021

APPALACHIAN WITNESS

Coeditors: Sherry Cook Stanforth (Managing Editor),
    Jim Minick & Dana Wildsmith
Book Reviews Editor: Linda Parsons

Layout & Design: Elizabeth H. Murphy - Illusion Studios
    Typeset in Adobe Garamond Pro, American Typewriter & Gabriola
Editorial Interns: Alyssa Dowdell & Margaret Dredger
Administrative/Editorial Assistant: Pamela Hirschler
Founding Editor: Jim Webb
Founding Publisher: Robb Webb

PMS&G logo courtesy of Colleen Anderson of *Mother Wit*
Front Cover: *Blossom* by Greg Clary; Photograph first
published in *Hole in the Head Review* (Volume 2, Issue 3)

Published in cooperation with Dos Madres Press

DOS MADRES

www.dosmadres.com

Dos Madres Press, Inc. is an Ohio Not For Profit Corporation
and a 501(c)(3) qualified public charity.
Contributions are tax deductible.

This project was supported in part by Johnson Controls
Foundation Matching Gift Program and anonymous donors.

ISBN 978-1-953252-40-1
Library of Congress Control Number: 2021946149

For ordering and information contact:
pmsg.journal@gmail.com.

PINE MOUNTAIN SAND & GRAVEL CO.
Whitesburg, Kentucky

NAME _____

For Period Ending _____, 195____

Earnings	No. Of	Rate	Amount
Tons ⓟ			
Hours ⓞ			
Hours @			
	Total Earnings		

DEDUCTIONS	AMOUNT	
Cash		
W'holding Tax		
S. S. Tax		
Fuel		
U. M. W. of A.		
Supplies		
Transfers		

Total Deductions		
AMOUNT DUE		
Overdraft		
TOTAL DUE EMPLOYEE		
Amount Due Company		

Received of Pine Mountain Sand & Gravel Co..
amount shown above in full payment for wages.

Signed: _____

This Check Includes Your
Vacation Pay Bonus.

"Don't worry about the mule going blind, just load the wagon"

TABLE
OF
CONTENTS

Book Reviews & News

About the
SOUTHERN APPALACHIAN
WRITERS COOPERATIVE

In 1974, a group of writers and activists gathered at Highlander Center in New Market, Tennessee, to form what became the Southern Appalachian Writers Cooperative. From its very beginning, SAWC was intended to support writers in our efforts to take control of our regional identity and to take action, individually and collectively, on the issues that impact our land and our people.

For over four decades, the Southern Appalachian Writers Cooperative has provided a place for us to come together to share our work and our struggles, and to ponder how these things affect, not only our work, but also our relationships with each other, with the region and with the broader culture. During the 1970s, SAWC sponsored readings and published *New Ground,* an anthology of contemporary Appalachian literature. In the 1980s, the Appalachian Poetry Project, initiated by Gurney Norman with poets George Ella Lyon and Bob Henry Baber, brought new life into SAWC. Poets and writers from throughout the Appalachian region gathered in their own and one another's communities and celebrated together at Highlander Center. SAWC has met (almost) annually since this time, usually at Highlander Research and Education Center and always in the fall. Through this and other SAWC Writers Gatherings and by sponsoring local readings and the literary magazine *Pine Mountain Sand & Gravel,* the Southern Appalachian

Writers Cooperative continues its original mission to foster community, activism and publication among Appalachia's writers.

Pine Mountain Sand & Gravel was founded in the mid-1980s by brothers Jim and Robb Webb. Their company, Appalapple Productions (Jim being a resident of Letcher County, Kentucky, and Robb of the Big Apple) produced three volumes of the journal before passing the torch to the Southern Appalachian Writers Cooperative in 1996. In its thirty-some years of publication, *PMS&G* has produced 24 volumes of contemporary Appalachian writing, and has been stewarded by 14 editors and co-editors. (Starting with Volume 19, young editorial interns also joined the team, reflecting the SAWC value for literary mentorship.) In 2015, the Southern Appalachian Writers Cooperative (in collaboration with Dos Madres Press) also published *Quarried: Three Decades of Pine Mountain Sand & Gravel*. Edited by editor emeritus Richard Hague, *Quarried* showcases early writing by notable Appalachian authors including Lee Howard, George Ella Lyon, Jeff Daniel Marion, Jim Wayne Miller and Gurney Norman, alongside newer work by many of Appalachia's currently established and emerging poets, essayists, and novelists.

Pine Mountain Sand & Gravel is now an annual, themed journal. The current call for submissions, purchase information, a list of upcoming readings, and information about the Southern Appalachian Writers Cooperative's fall and other gatherings can always be found at *sawconline. net*. You may also contact *Pine Mountain Sand & Gravel* at pmsg.journal@gmail.com.

INTRODUCTION

I once saw twin albino fawns grazing alongside their brown mother in a neighborhood field. The surprising rupture to my sense of "the normal" stopped me on my path. One of these ghostly creatures lived to be a yearling, appearing (camouflaged at last!) in a frozen drift beneath February's Snow Moon. Again, wonder compelled me to be still—to watch, listen, and earnestly ponder the mysteries of creation. I waited in the cold silence of my car until the deer finally disappeared. Today, I continue to tell the story of witnessing a biological rarity in my home meadow—and how that small moment expanded interpretations for how I might *be* in the world.

In October of 2020, Volume 23 emerged between hard slices of pandemic mortality and sociopolitical violence. Pauletta Hansel's wise introduction noted that while *PMS&G* writers "could scarcely imagine the many edges" suddenly carving into our lives, we willingly conducted meaningful work from inside the fray, crafting richly textured interpretations of self, family, community, region, country, and world. Now, here is Volume 24. We stand as witness inside these present times to again reveal our bewilderment and our awe...our unbound truths and facts...our varying revelations. The stories and testimonies within these pages provide evidence that the Appalachian imagination will continue to sing far above the noise of tampering forces, declaring and celebrating in diverse tones its case for existence.

Sherry Cook Stanforth
Summer, 2021

This issue of *Pine Mountain Sand & Gravel* is dedicated to our founding publisher and friend, Robb Webb, 1939-2021.

Kevin Rippin

No Nothing

The thing they did then is the thing they do now.
If they worked at Bethlehem Steel then,
they work at Bethlehem Steel now.
If they taught school at Cypress Elementary then,
they teach school at Cypress Elementary now.
Only the tense has changed, and it has changed
only because we've changed it. We don't blame them.
They had no idea they would die. They have no idea
they're dead. We like to think they're alive,
will climb the front steps and be home for dinner,
Only the time changes and the time changes
only because we've changed it. We keep changing time
because changing time is what keeps them alive.
We can't forget about them for even one day
because if we forget about them for even one day,
one day turns into two days, two days turns into four,
turns into months, turns into years. If they are forgotten,
they eventually die. If they die, there's no working
in the mill, no mill, no teaching school, no school,
no dinner, no town, no them. If there's no them,
there's no us. If there's no us, there's no nothing,
& if there's no nothing, that's no good.

Jacob Strautmann

Nostos

The unwound yards of insulation — a ground-dweller
    dragged before nesting frissoned in its earshape
    the last day it longed for others — lay a strip of
    bright yellow in the July sun, lifting, settling for
    the wind.

The trailer skirts let go, and hornets swarm the
    unfastening men with flashlights up the crude
    stowage, wheels rounding twenty years of dry-
    rot refit by supper. They are taking my boyhood
    home. Nothing forever.

When the hitch slips in, a small tractor torques like a
    green horse for the weight, bucks throttle,
    bucks attempts to budge the ancient mobile
    home. Then a man grips the grill, ties himself
    outstretched, beautifully counterbalances

140 lbs. to odyssey it all away. His body a prow steady
    in the gale as the surprised ship lurches over the
    roiling fields of hay — he doesn't say five words,
    but he's our poem, Master Thief, and then some.

Connie Jordan Green

Witness

They smoke beneath a side canopy
or sheltered by the passageway
between classrooms and gym.
They are not bad, only wild
with the fierceness of youth,
reckless on hormones and longing.
In later years they will marry,
own their own garage or teach
math to boys as rebellious
as they once were. For now
they cup their hands to tent
the match against the wind, inhale
morning's first taste of nicotine,
exhale a cloud that settles on clothing
and in hair, scent that clings
through English, history classes,
where girls in starched white blouses
move to the far side of the room,
secretly eye the rebels
while they feign attention to the text
before them, bid the dreams
sleep will bring, their own
wildness a banked fire, embers
glowing in the dark, waiting
for love's warm breath.

Diana Becket

Debt

She smears dirt and condensation
down the kitchen window lit
by the red-orange sunset—
rinses the cloth with the dishes piled
in the greasy sink. Her ears strain
to catch her children's shouts,
eyes focus on clouds that move,
dark against the skyline.

Limbs caged by pain,
she struggles to bend for mugs
on the floor and lift plates
from the table to soak in water.
She craves the pills for release
into numb tunnels but dreads
when they spit her out
into dark caverns.

A slammed door muffles
her children's screams. She tries
to leave the window but pauses
to listen. As the cries fade
to muttering, she turns
back to the sink.

She cleans pans, watches
town lights break
into night.

Michelle Boettcher

Kitchen Tools

Digital Photograph

Jordan Laney

The Matron

She always wore Maybelline mascara
the pink and green kind. Spreading
Duke's thick on sandwiches, kept in the Frigidaire.
Woodsmoke-filled living room, dark morning bus rides
along Rural Route 5, *Why'd You Come In Here Lookin' Like That*
belting through speakers. Afternoons plucking bloodroot
behind the chicken pens, red finger trails
shucking hair off corn, while worms fall to the porch.
Reminded of her hot temper and the stubborn silence
while cooking hotdogs and macaroni.

She whispers, *God don't like ugly*
when I start to brag. Reminding me
pretty is as pretty does
when I stand in front of the mirror too long
preparing for altar calls, sunrise services
followed by chocolate gravy and green bean casserole.

I am the easiest secret she carries—
skipping school to smoke rabbit tobacco
stealing cars and falling in love
the names of children she doesn't have.
White lies etched into my very being,
brown eyes reminding her of where
she has been, and hope delivered.

Stephanie Kendrick

Women Who Lived in Me

The holler girl jumps too fast
into muddy rivers, into muscular arms,
knows her feet may never touch
the ground, holds her breath too long.

The girl with bloodshot eyes screams
into her own ears, to the bottom of her throat
until she is so full of her own words, she floats
away, a balloon lost to the clouds.

The displaced hustler shows up to class
in work uniform, with early wrinkles
and the smell of strangers. She buries debt in holes,
and learns to love the dirt underneath her nails.

The spray-tanned goddess uses too much
eyeliner to contour maps of every mistake
she makes across her face. She warns
everyone she meets, without saying one word.

All these young women, fueled
by boiling blood and jagged tongues.
Unaware,
the cocoons will not hold them forever.

Courtney Barnoski

Hellions

we'd hide our acid tabs
in our maxi pads

take 'em down to the river
wave at barges drenchin' their way through

No tellin' about
the stamps bleeding ink on our tongues

we'd inhale, watching the sky bend
exhale, then stumble in

we'd obsess over the still water
float until our bodies collapsed

we'd sprout gills n fins
shapeshift n spin

we'd lay low with catfish—
watch crawdads

reminisce over days
when we too was prey

crawl around in our skin
fantasize about trazodone n Vicodin

watch light's twisted curves
lay low to hear grass breathe

we'd feel the earth turn
cosmic kids, raised by the stars

we'd close our eyes
swearing we could see the future

make our own family
where no one felt alone

run away from our parents—
stay in shacks n shanties

we'd use old spray paint
to write handsome things on each others' arms

cover our wounds
with glitter n Dollar Tree band-aids

vowing to love each other
'pon our hearts, swear to God

we'd stay sober n clean
successful n fed

though we was no-count—
we was just a bunch of hellions

Pamela Hirschler

Good Intentions

Anything free won't fit, or at least that's the wisdom
I gleaned as a girl when a cardboard box of clothes arrived
from an older cousin. Her proportions never matched
my own, and the styles—too recent to be vintage—
brought unwanted attention on the playground.

But even those hand-me-downs were passed on
again, dropped in a donation box, then washed
and gathered with new testament bibles and used toys
cleaned and repaired for a Christmas charity project.
We took them across the railroad tracks and up the holler
to the coal-camp meeting house one hundred twenty steps
up the mountain from the gravel parking lot, (I counted).
In winter, the black coal stove stood hot in the center
of the one room, in summer, funeral home fans fluttered
like butterflies from green plank pews in the sticky breeze.

We taught from lightly-used Sunday school books donated
every quarter from the town church, played the upright piano
(how did it get up there?), and then later that spring, something
that nests in your brain like a snake, a childhood memory, a girl
clutching a doll with a patched dress, learning about baby Jesus
in March, the forsythia blooming, maybe some Easter eggs
hidden on the grounds, the manger in her book already colored in.

Elizabeth Bailey

Pantoum of the Great Society

Mud Creek, Kentucky, was dirt poor,
stripped of energy for union battles,
stripped of coal. Families fought
over each other's Valium vials.

Stripped of energy for union battles
men picked steel strings, wives put up beans,
fought over Valium vials, years
after Johnson declared war on poverty.

Men picked steel strings, wives put up beans.
They gathered on porches; the moon rose;
years after Johnson declared war on poverty
and introduced the Great Society on the grainy TV.

They gathered on porches; the moon rose;
Children got a Head Start, their parents more drugs.
Johnson announced the Great Society.
Some left. Others swallowed the bitter pills.

Children got a Head Start, their parents more drugs.
Old men spit their black lungs into bandanas.
Some left. Others swallowed the bitter pills.
Depression passed down like a family heirloom.

Old men spit their black lungs into bandanas.
Clinton declared the War on Poverty won.
Depression passed down like a family heirloom.
Young men signed up for Iraq, some came back.

Clinton declared the War on Poverty won,
union songs confined to vinyl, then CDs.
Young men signed up for Iraq, some came back
to fight crystal meth and crack.

There are no union mines in East Kentucky.
Stripped of coal, stripped of desire,
families abandoned to unemployment and drugs.
Mud Creek, Kentucky, is still dirt poor.

Michael Henson

The Scratch-Off Man

By the third day, the Boy began to worry over how to get food and drinkable water. He and his sister had run away from foster care and were headed north to Ohio to find their mother, hiding out by day and hiking through the woods and fields by night. He was twelve, she was just six; it was a lot of responsibility. He hadn't figured it would take so long and he did not know how long they still had to go. Had they crossed into Kentucky yet? Or were they still in Tennessee?

He couldn't tell and it was one more worry.

He had learned about survival in the woods from his foster care home school, so when they left, they were mostly ready. They had some power bars. They had purification tablets and a filtering water bottle. They had some money. But now, everything was running low. And he was tired of the whining.

Sissy did not whine much, but when she did, it went on for miles. There was plenty to whine about. They were both eaten up with mosquito bites and chiggers. Bug spray—they had forgotten to bring along bug spray. They were both hungry most of the time, both thirsty. They ate up their sandwiches the first day. The power bars were getting low. And, to make it all worse, he had managed to get them lost.

They had kept close to the northbound Interstate, either by sight or by sound. But at a cloverleaf interchange, he had taken a wrong turn. So now, they were trudging down a lonesome country road, hoping it would lead them back to the Interstate.

And it did. The boy heard the sweep of cars on the pavement and the grumble of the big trucks. He could see the rise in the surface of the road as it passed over the highway. Even better, on the other side of the overpass, he could see the outline of a store, lit up like it was its own small city.

"Look, Sissy," he said. "It's a store." It was the perfect sort of store, with the gas pumps out front and a little bit of everything inside.

Sissy said nothing, but he sensed that she brightened at the notion. They picked up the pace, but halfway across the overpass, he stopped. Fifty yards down the highway, a big, black, digital signboard with bright red letters read *Amber Alert*. As he watched, the big red letters flashed off and smaller letters displayed their names and described the two of them as missing.

He stared through another cycle of their Amber Alert; Sissy asked, "What's it say?"

"It says, when we get to the store, you need to wait outside."

But she did not want to be left alone to wait outside. "No," she said. "I want to go in with you." She pouted at the thought all the way to the edge of the lot.

They stopped in the shadow of a logging truck where the floodlights of the parking lot would not reach. "You wait here," he said.

She responded with a low wail, something animal, fearful, and sly. He was afraid someone would hear the whining and that someone would have seen their names on the highway and the whining would draw their attention. By himself, he was not so much of a target. No one would think much of a kid of twelve coming in by himself to buy snacks, drinks, and the makings of sandwiches.

But if he had to drag her behind him, sniffling and all a-whimper, that would set off alarms. Somebody would have seen the Amber Alert; somebody would want to be a hero; somebody would call the sheriff.

He paused a moment to think.

"Okay, Sissy. Here's what we'll do." He was sure now he had it figured out. "We'll go to the store together, but you're gonna wait outside and guard the backpacks. Okay?"

"Why can't I come inside the store with you?"

"Cause we don't want people to see us together."

"Why . . ?"

"Cause they'll know we ran away."

"Why . . . ?

"Cause they're looking for a boy and girl together. Older boy, little girl. Like us. See? And if they catch us, we'll have to go back to foster care."

She pondered this a moment, then put out her hand to go with him to the door of the store.

In the shadow around the corner of the store, he said, "Okay, here's where you wait for me."

Her eyes opened wide and he sensed that she was about to start wailing again.

"Okay, Sissy, okay. Here's what we'll do. We'll go up to the door together, but you're gonna wait outside where they can't see you and you're gonna guard the backpacks. Okay?"

"Why can't I come in the store with you?"

"Cause we don't want people to see us together."

"Why . . ?"

"I already told you. Cause they'll know we ran away and then they'll call the police and then we'll have to go back."

"Why . . ?"

"Cause they're looking for a boy and a girl together. Older boy, little girl. Remember?"

Finally, she agreed to wait if he brought her some cookies. The whole front of the store was glass, but most of the glass was covered with posters advertising beer or ice cream. "Just wait here where they can't see you. And don't look inside, cause then they will."

He knew that she would look inside, but he hoped that the people in the store wouldn't see her. Maybe they wouldn't be looking her way. Or maybe they would see her, but they wouldn't put the two of them together in their minds.

All he could do was hope for the best. There was no other way, not if they were going to get what they needed from this store.

He tried to keep it simple; he tried to make it quick. Bug spray. A loaf of bread. A jar of peanut butter. A jar of strawberry jam. Two six-packs of apple juice, the kind that comes in a little box with a straw you use as a spear to get into the juice. She liked those. And some more power bars, half a dozen more power bars in different flavors. A power bar made a breakfast; another one made a lunch. Then peanut butter and jelly sandwiches for supper; they would be supper and dessert all in one. What else? What else? What else do we need? The cookies! He knew she liked Oreos and grabbed a pack from off the shelf.

He clutched the peanut butter jar and the jam jar

and the cartons of juice in the crook of his left elbow, then set the cookies on top of these and stacked the power bars, one after the other, in a pyramid on top of the cookies and the loaf of bread on top of that. The bug spray came in a slick plastic bottle, so he clutched it in his left hand. He spread his right hand over the stack of power bars and bread to hold everything in place and headed for the counter. He glanced toward the door. Sure enough, Sissy stood leaning into the glass panel at the side of the door with her hands over her eyes so she could peer inside.

The boy made a subtle motion of his head to wave his sister back from the door. Other than that, he tried not to look in her direction. *Move away*, he thought. *Please just move away.* But he could tell by a side-eye glance that she continued to peer in the window.

A big man in a ball cap, t-shirt, and jeans was the only person ahead of him in line. The man had just bought a fistful of scratch-off lottery tickets and he scratched through each one with a dime pinched in his fingers.

Sissy continued to peer through the window. The clerk had dark-tone skin and black, black hair. He looked over Sissy's way, but if he registered any thought or emotion at all, it was boredom.

"Ten more," said the man in line.

The clerk took the man's money, rang up the purchase, counted ten more scratch-off tickets off the roll, snatched the tickets off the roll, snapped the receipt off the machine, and handed over receipt, tickets, and change, all in a single, swift, practiced motion.

By the time the man scratched off the ten new

tickets, the clerk had shaken off his boredom. He looked beyond the man scratching off his tickets and noticed the boy struggling to hold onto his armload of purchases. "That's it, man," he said to the scratch-off man. "I got to cut you off."

The scratch-off man looked up in shock. The boy stood behind him and a little to the side; he could see the sweat that had beaded on the man's temple.

"No, you can't do that," the man told the clerk.

"I can, and I'm doing it."

"No, you can't. I know my rights."

"And I know mine. I can cut you off if I think you're out of control."

"Out of control? I'm not out of control."

"You look out of control to me."

The boy's left arm was getting tired. The pyramid of power bars was threatening to slide. His grip on the jars had begun to slip; if he shifted, he would flatten the air out of the bread. His sister, by the door, stamped her foot and frowned.

The scratch-off man's hand began to shake. "You can't do this, man," he said. "I know my rights."

"And I know mine. I have other customers waiting."

"You have got to be kidding me."

The clerk folded his arms. "Do I look like I'm kidding?"

"This is some kind of joke."

"Can you please step aside? I need to help this young man check out his items."

"I'm not stepping anywhere. This is a joke."

The clerk motioned to the boy to step forward.

But the scratch-off man stepped in front of the

boy to block his path. "I'm not done," he said to the clerk. "I was here first."

"You're done."

"And who says?"

"I say."

"Well, I need to talk to your supervisor."

"You're talking to the supervisor."

"Well, then I want the manager."

"I'm the manager. And I'm the boss. And I'm the owner. And I'm the one who decides when to cut somebody off which is what I'm doing, cutting you off. Now . . ."

The boy tried again to step around the Scratch-Off Man, but again, the man blocked him. The pyramid of power bars had collapsed. The boy managed to catch them before they fell to the floor, but at the cost of crushing the bread against his chest.

The clerk signaled the boy to bring his things to the counter. But when the boy tried to place the peanut butter jar near the cash register, the Scratch-Off Man put out his hand to block him. "No, you don't," he said. "Put everything right over here. I'm still talking to Mister Supervisor."

The clerk, who was really the supervisor and the manager and the owner and the boss and the one who decides, reached for the peanut butter and the boy tried slide it across the counter. But the Scratch-Off Man leaned across, snatched the jar, and handed it back to the boy. "Don't worry," he said. "I got this." He pulled a couple of crisp bills from his wallet. "I got this," he said again. "You go on," he said to the boy. "Take your stuff. I got this."

The clerk raised one finger. "Just a moment," he said.

The Scratch-Off Man said, "Go on." He did not look back at the boy. "I'll pay for what you got. I got plenty of good American money. I'll pay for your bit of groceries. You just go on. Me and this rag-head got some business to settle."

The Clerk pulled a phone from his pocket while the Scratch-Off Man told the boy about his Rights and Being an American. He told the boy, It's My Money and I'll Do What I Want with It. He told him, Know Your Rights and told him Don't Let These Foreigners Tell You What You Can Do With Your Own Money?

Meanwhile, the Clerk who was also the Supervisor and was also the Owner and the Boss and the Manager and the One Who Decides was busy on the phone. "Yes," he said. "I have a customer who won't leave and he's disrupting the other customers." And, "Yes, I feel threatened." And, "No, he doesn't appear to have a weapon." He pressed the phone between his ear and shoulder and pulled a plastic bag from beneath the counter. He handed it to the boy, and signaled him to bag up his things and go.

The Scratch-Off Man leaned into the counter and jabbed a finger at the clerk. He continued to speak of his Rights and of his pockets full of Good American Money that he could spend just as he pleased. He was still speaking of his Rights, his God-Given Constitutional Rights as the boy slipped out the door to where his sister waited, wide-eyed and hungry.

Richard Hague

Mr. MAGA Tours the Former Eden

Ain't no way this rose
is real, and the color
of it—fake news. And
that Shasta daisy—
floozie, show-off, primadonna.
I'd say give me that
sulk of poison ivy
under the camellias,
that snakelet of ground ivy
across the back lawn.
I'll take that sprizz
of nettles in the zinnias—
and hell, I love that bindweed,
the way it'll trip up any wannabe King,
crawl up any Queen's or First Lady's dress.

Gaby Bedetti

A Picnic Remembered

1. Evidence

The day after his arrest, he told a fellow inmate
he had researched ways to dispose of a body in acid.
The guards found his list of three possible reasons
for her blood to have been in his trunk.

With the discovery of the blood,
my colleague—who sat with me at graduation
in full regalia, who joked with me as we walked
through the campus ravine, and was widely supported
for promotion—was charged with murdering his wife.

A mushroom hunter found her bones in a ditch.
More evidence was collected:
The smell of gunpowder led to the weapon
in the attic. The blood he thought he had
scrubbed away had pooled in a crevice.

2. His Family

I had seen the family months before she went missing,
seated under the shelter at the department picnic.
His wife and five-year-old were wearing top knots,
their heads bent together over a plate of potato chips,
her cellphone with its recorded fights out of sight.

He was sitting across from them, looking away,
indifferent to the child who displayed
his father's jug ears. The hand wearing the wedding band
rested on one knee; the other was cupped on the table.
He had left his brass knuckles at home.

Hilda Downer

Boomerang

Summer's overgrown tendrils
search for anything to grasp onto
in a rare photo of me as a teenager.

Out of a foster home,
a stowaway among relatives and friends,
I stand at my grandparents' house,
abandoned by paint and death.
I have no place to go
except college.

The huge boxwood bounces me back
after I stumble into its hard arms,
trying to escape having my photo taken.
Though Whitman steadies me,
I believe I am uglier
than the elephant man.

Now, to only be on the brink
of so many mistakes,
and to look as I did then,
I could not guide me.

I had too much freedom.
A starved panther,
I could barely pinch my skin
to give insulin injections.

In the image,
stillness is my survival skill.
I strain to hear
my own voice from the future.

"I will remember you,"
I say to myself
in a boomerang of time
I catch now.

Pauletta Hansel

Safe as Sand

From lines in Muriel Rukeyser's 1938 *The Book of the Dead,*
in the spirit of a "golden shovel."

Was it dusty?
Lord, yes.
We'd drive our trucks through glittered clouds.
But no need to worry; you could eat a pound a day,
they told us. No masks either.
It would look bad for tourists headed out to the lake.
Most days we'd laugh it away. Coal ash flu.
Our skin flaked off like fish scales.
Of course, they knew.
I never saw one of them sucking in the dust.
But workers? We were birds blown out of the mine.
They tested the fish for arsenic.
Not us. We made a shrine up by the plant for those already dead
from the cancer—liver, brain, leukemia. My wife,
she lays a penny there, says this is more than what we're worth
to those who own this Tennessee Valley.

Sources:
August 28, 2019 AP report, https://abcnews.go.com/Health/wireStory/
tva-backlash-grows-coal-ash-spill-workers-fall-65234169
https://www.nationalgeographic.com/environment/2019/02/coal-other-
dark-side-toxic-ash/
 Rukeyser lines embedded in the poem: "No masks. / Most of them were
not from this valley"

Les Brown

Corona Spring

The truck stops beside a pile of dead limbs
where I placed them by the road.
Unmasked men shove them into grinding jaws,
spew them into the hot truck box.
The masked woman next door
pushes her mower into overgrown grass,
clippings lying in her wake
to decay in warm summer days ahead.
The neighborhood lawns are better tended
this Coronavirus Season.

We wave at each other from our secure distance
as men stack bodies into refrigerated trucks,
morgues, beyond Times Square's lights.
The masked, gloved and gowned
pump air into dying with hope of resurrections.
I see the graphs, numbers, projections,
hear accounts from homebound commentators,
and spins from the White House of Mirrors
pronouncing progress to the world.
We cut, stack, burn and bury our refuse.

Sam Campbell

Self-Portrait in a Zoom Call

They call it the cancellation culture: love but no weddings, deaths but no funerals; birthdays pass without regard, the congregation has no mass, and scholars cannot commence.

Living room walls, white concrete block like schoolhouse rooms and prison cells—not an ideal backdrop for poetry class. Bedroom blackout curtains, dark grey, damper office visits. Try on artificial backdrops like swimsuits I'll buy but never wear— country sunrise, blood-spattered asphalt, clichéd beach scene. Close out—the backdrop options remain in folders unused like bikinis with the tags still attached. I settle for cold cement and wait for a pelican to scoop me up in his gular and fly me back to the old realities.

Buttons are now required to turn myself on. One turns off my invisibility. Another gives me a voice. I thought I'd know when I became a cyborg; thought there would be more initiation than app installation. Thought there'd be more revolt from the masses. Now I wonder if we weren't already there.

Technology resurrects, saves us from isolation in the Time of the Quarantine. We see those who are there, hear words not spoken to our faces. But these are merely ghosts of people we know.

Boxed people climb into their computers at scheduled times, their pigmants pixelate, eye blur by poor connection, voices crack across wi-fi signals floatign invisible in the atmosphere. Gallery view shows each face like portraits in museums we can no longer meander. It wasn't until now I see the art beneath each framed face; see the life behind the body. My professor's white cat struts across his square; a classmate's gray braids, and another's lipstick-red eyeglasses; another comforts his newborn in a dark corner, far away from the screen.

I never speak to others now; I talk only to myself. My face stares back at me as I converse and I make eye contact with my own greens, watch the way my lips curve around words, carefully carve out an appropriate smile, positioned just so—

Gaby Bedetti
Pigeon on a Cross
Digital Photograph

Kirsten Reneau

The Big Bang

In my sixth-grade science class, Mrs. O'Neal said that she wasn't going to teach us about the big bang because she was a Christian and she didn't believe in that. She believed in one god, in Adam and Eve, in snakes and gardens and trees the bore fruits made of knowledge. Marissa sat next to me and we traded looks that couldn't be recreated with language, but the closest thing would have been *Yikes*.

I'm sure that if I ever told my mom about that class, Mrs. O'Neal would have gotten in some kind of trouble (because mom, I'm sure, would have told Dad, and Dad would have told my Uncle Jim, who was the principal of the middle school.) But it doesn't matter because I didn't tell her.

We were thinking about other things. Space, our creation—it all drifted to the back of our minds. Marissa and I spent most of our time creating cootie catchers that would tell us our fortune, twisting apple stems to find the names of the men we'd marry, preparing for the trips we'd be taking over the upcoming Christmas break. I wanted to believe that possibility that the magic could be true. We lived in the hidden mountains of West Virginia and we were much more interested in the magic of what was coming next, how we were going to get out of our small town and see the world, than how it all came to be.

Christmas came and went, and we returned to school in the early, bitter cold of January. Just days before we started class again, the Sago Mine disaster happened, and then no one in school learned anything about space at all; we sat in science class every day, the room cold and sharp, and just watched the news. We served as witnesses, looking for faces we recognized, trying to see if the men we knew were still breathing. Sago was an hour from my hometown, and Marissa's dad was one of the miners we were searching for on the TV.

For thirteen days, thirteen minors were stuck underground. We counted the days, counted the men hidden in the dirt of the earth. No one wanted to admit that thirteen was unlucky, that suddenly we were all more superstitious than we actually wanted to be. One of the miners that died always wrote "Jesus Saves" in the coal dust of the mine car before it descended downwards, the news said. Mrs. O'Neal didn't say anything about god after that but, as we waited for the reporters to pronounce the mine a mass grave, she'd hold her hands clasped together in front of her, as if she was praying.

Marissa was out of school all that first week, and then the week after, and then the week after that, and then we didn't see her again. She disappeared into the darkness of whatever was on the other side of a death that's not your own. All the miners but one died; the twelve funerals were held back-to-back on one Sunday, where they were put back into the earth that had smothered them dead. At the mine, twelve black satin bows sat outside, stained dark and damp from the falling snow.

Marissa wasn't the first person I knew with a coal miner for a father, but she was the first person I knew who had family officially die from it. Of course, there was black lung, where the inside of the body becomes darker than a tar pit, but we considered that more of a second-hand coal mine related death rather than a direct one. This death though—it was different.

31

But that's why me and everyone else in sixth grade that year never learned about the big bang, not formally. I didn't feel like I missed out. When the sky turned black each night, I imagined that it all came from that mine cracked open, the darkness leaking out and suffocating us all. It didn't matter to me how we got here; I had finally learned how it all ended.

Rhonda Pettit

A Former Slave Teaches
New Math to Someone

Hello. I live in a small town called Divisible.
When Someone asks where I was born, I say: in Divisible.
When Someone says, I can't find that town on a map,
    I say: It's on my map.
When Someone says, Are you calling me a liar, I say:
    Do you know how to read?
When Someone says, Show me the map with a town
    called Divisible, I say:
Look at me. I am in Divisible. I never moved away.
When Someone says, you are not a map, I say: Look at me.
My body is a town.
My body has a history.
My blood the map of the roads
I travelled, the rose of the word
I sing.
When Someone says, I don't understand, I say:
I am here.
You are here.
We are in Divisible.
When Someone says, I don't understand you, I say:
    I know know   know.
That's why we've never moved away.
You are alive, I am alive
in Divisible.

When Someone walks away, and says nothing, I call that
    long division.

Michael Garrigan

7th Anthracite Coal District
of Pennsylvania

The Lord gives us mountains
and we fail to mine out that grandness.
—Anders Carlson-Wee

Victor Augustine was declared competent to be a miner
in the Seventh Anthracite Coal District Mines of this great
Commonwealth on the 20th day of May 1905.

Twenty years later, just before his death under dark rock,
his son Albert Augustine was declared competent to be a miner
in this great Commonwealth on the 20th Day of June 1925.

I met Albert, Poppy, as he was dying. Something with his lungs,
dark rock slowly collapsing onto him from inside each of his breaths.
Poppy was the last miner of rock in our family, the last
to dig deep into the dark and to let coal dust cover his skin.

The fissures of his shovel strike against shale and siltstone
reverberate in our lungs, crack in our ribs, crumble
into dust shavings settling at the back of our throats,
each of us still miners of the 7th Anthracite Coal District
        mapping our way under bedrock,
            reaching into dark caverns for seeds of rock,
                seeds of watershed, seeds of light
                blessing this geology of our genealogy.

Anna Egan Smucker

The Enemy

Dipping fish sticks in tartar sauce, mushing
   boiled potatoes around on our plates, happy
   there's no long division, diagramming, or memorizing
   catechism before Sunday afternoon.

"Dad? Tell us another story about the war."
   He looks apologetically at Mom who just wants
   the dishes washed, her kitchen in order, or maybe
   just doesn't care to be reminded of those years.

But Dad . . . folds his napkin, sips his tea, sighs, begins…
   "That darkness, that fog, so thick, that easy
   for a plane to get that lost, and crash.
And the pilot, off-course, blind, so young.

Midnight, Doc woke me
   and for hours, we tried, we *tried*.
Me handing him instruments…praying.
Maybe both of us. Sometimes prayers helped?

They didn't that night on Amchitka.
That poor boy, that bad, that much blood.
No ID. Impossible
   to know who to contact in Japan."

Lenten Friday, 1958

Robert Beveridge

Nine of Pentacles (Reversed)

Oh, more of this, now? Have we
found ourselves in a place where
even a two-tone Chevy, a half-pack
of Marlboros, and a butterscotch
milkshake is somehow not enough
to afford you entrance to the VFW
parking lot on a Tuesday dinnertime?

The whole town's there, hoods up,
old men in vinyl lawn chairs, ladies
in gingham and calico, and the high
schoolers, the bodyshoppers,
the bohunks, the maintenance
guys all in their pompadours, best
jeans, on the prowl, forever on the prowl.

And here I am in the driver's seat
and I gotta ask myself before I pull in
when it is that you go from jeans
to madras, when you trade beer
for lemonade, your cocked hip
against your cruiser for your lawn
chair in the twilight. I wonder

what dad thought of this
retirement plan, whether he thinks
at all, after the blowup at the mill
put him in the ground three years
ago. I wonder if there's something
else outside these city limits.

Jessica Weyer Bentley

Shooting Off the Solid
Ode to the 1981 Tater Branch Mine Disaster

That December day in '81 you were tired of swallowing coal.
So you walked out into the cold incandescent light of day,
to eat the lunch she carefully tied up for you.
Fried bologna and white bread.
Dead man walking.
She knew what coal meant.
She came from coal.
Her bones were charred with it—
lymphoma.
She still waved you on past the hot tracks and coal gons,
down to the veins of black.
But back in '81 on Tater Branch an angel hitched with you.
You just cleared the drift mouth when it blew.
Collapsing you to your knees—
praying.
Just like Vietnam.
Black suet flew instead of tank shrapnel.
Eight men were dead.
You spoke the truth to those dark stiff suits.
Walking in tall with black rimmed eyes and nails.
No other union mines would come to call.
That act of grace got you black-balled
and government cheese.
Yet, it taught your boys to stand up for the dead,
unless they shoot at you.
These winter nights your insomnia holds vigil.
Their ore-scuffed hands waken you.
Your sniper fire wakens you.
Her distant whispers ache in you.

Jack Wright

The Incident at An Lao River: 1967

Memories are bullets.
Some whiz by and only spook you.
Others tear you open and leave you in pieces
-Richard Kadrey

At first light I arose and stepped out of the tent, recalling my orders for the day. We had slept for weeks in a graveyard where we set up camp, fortified our tents with sandbags and set up a shower and latrine among the red clay mounds. Beneath the mounds rested the bones of the holy ones, holy to the Vietnamese Buddhists who worshiped their ancestors. Several colorful open-air altars where incense had once burned remained standing among rows of graves. Now, the First Air Cavalry tactical operations center lived here on the edge of Landing Zone Two Bits, the airfield next to this sacred boneyard. Vietnamese families could no longer visit to honor their dead, as had been their long-standing custom.

I passed through the maze of grave sites and took in a deep breath to let my mind clear, another day closer to my exit from a war zone. I saw sunrays growing across the valley and into the surrounding mountains. The steep green slopes reminded me of home, but instead of coal strip mine benches and overburden, long swaths of brown defoliated trails revealed Agent Orange's destructive paths.

As I walked to the mess tent, helicopters here and there began the whomp-whomp-whomp warm-up for take-off. First thing after breakfast I showered, one of the few luxuries offered at the landing zone besides beer at 10 cents a can. The shower was a canvas Australian shower bag hanging from a homemade scaffold constructed of wooden ammunition crates. Early morning sunshine made the trickle of water solar heated. With only 58 days left in Vietnam I was looking forward to a real bath.

Later that day my pal Harry and I picked up a jeep at Military Police headquarters. We drove to the prisoner of war compound and hooked up a long trailer behind the jeep. The topless open-sided trailer held plenty of room for several prisoners. Harry loaded in a bale of empty sandbags. We picked up four foxhole entrenching tools from a nearby outbuilding. The humid afternoon would reach into the nineties, a hot time to venture to the river for prisoners to fill sandbags and stack them back into the trailer. Harry and I walked to the POW guardhouse to pick up eight prisoners for the work detail.

We were in our early 20s. The prisoners were peasants, rice farmers, evacuated from their villages in the scenic, rice-rich and deadly An Lao River Valley. Their communities were being burned and leveled to turn the valley to a free fire zone in an attempt to keep rice away from the enemy.

Our eight charges were papasans, dressed in loose fitting pants and shirts, many with thin whiskers, some with rags wrapped around their heads. They were in their 40s or older; it was hard to tell. We herded them into the trailer.

It was the first time these rice farmers had been allowed outside the crowded concertina-wired compound since their evacuation. If they were suspected of being VC or NVA sympathizers, we were not informed. They were classified as low security risks, so they were not bound. They squatted freely, the eight of them, in the trailer, and we drove off, Harry at the wheel and me riding shotgun with my M-16 rifle and an army issue Colt .45 pistol. Harry's M-16 was tucked between the seats.

Palm trees canopied the red clay road, shading it from the growing heat. It was tunnel-like and dappled in places along the three-mile route. Trucks and small motorcycles peopled the road, coming and going. Three-wheeled Lambrettas, used as taxis with a covered carriage, often transported 15 or more—stuffed in tight—some hanging precariously from the sides. Kids played along the roadside and dogs barked. Women wearing full-length white dresses and tan conical hats trotted along the roadway with a long pole balanced across one shoulder. Suspended on each end of the pole was a plastic bucketful of water. These ladies bounced the buckets along steady and effortless, ballet like, headed back to their thatch-roofed mud huts.

When we reached the hamlet of Bong Son, traffic increased, so we slowed. I glanced back at the prisoners, worrying that someone might jump and run for it. I squeezed the grip of my rifle. But they continued talking among themselves and laughed occasionally, a nice outing for them after being held in captivity for weeks. Harry wheeled a right turn, passing several shops in the center of town. The sunny weather after monsoon season brought more folks out into the streets. We turned left just before we got to an icehouse and headed toward the working bridge. It was one of the two bridges across the river at the village. The Viet Cong had targeted the other bridge in October. A span blown down in the center section lay in the water like a domino leaning against the next bridge pillar.

Along the roadside a few banana trees grew out of the green plumage. Approaching the bridge, we turned left again and headed downhill to the sandy riverside beach. Stalks of pale-yellow grass grew out of the sandbars along the river. A few people were lounging in the sun, including some Korean soldiers—ROKs they were called—dressed sharply in starched and creased combat fatigues with the usual weapons, M-1 rifles and carbines.

We parked. Harry and I spoke very little Vietnamese, but the detainees got the message. Barefooted, they stepped into the dry sand. We handed out the shovels from the trailer and cut open the bale of empty sandbags for filling. They started work twenty feet from the water's edge. Four shoveling, four holding the bags open, taking turns, taking their time, tying and neatly stacking the bags into the nearby flatbed trailer.

Far across the An Lao River stood a vacant Catholic church with white plaster walls and a red tiled roof. The river flowed by, brown, wide and sluggish. Under the shadow of the bridge a fisherman skulled with one oar. On out a ways in the water, a skiff plowed along, moving with the current, leaving a small wake. A few clouds cottoned the sky. I glanced up toward the bridge when it began to hum and then tremble from the wheels of a long U.S. convoy coming into town. Military trucks towing artillery pieces, others loaded with supplies, and more with soldiers, their helmets bobbling as they crossed the way and moved toward their next assignment.

Harry and I sat in the sand as a warm wind rose up and purled from the river. We kept a watchful eye on the elderly men who seemed to be enjoying the work together. They chatted and laughed, never seeming to pay us any mind.

The papasans' bare backs streaked with sweat from working in the sun. We set out the water can and paper cups. After about an hour and a half of labor, I decided we had enough for a load of bags. We had them pack the tools and the leftover unused bags onto the trailer. I decided to let them take a bath in a pooled stream that fed the river off to our right. The water was shallow in that section but deep enough for a good immersion, so we could watch them more easily there. With no bath in the POW compound, they had not had the freedom to bathe in quite some time.

I pointed to the little pool of flowing water and scrubbed my hands up and down over my neck and face as if I were washing myself and pointed back to the pool. They began laughing and waded in with rolled up pant legs and embraced the water. After bathing they frolicked and splashed each other. I had been a lifeguard at Fort Sill back in Oklahoma, and memories from a more innocent time rushed back.

Finally, it was time to leave. I motioned the men to come in from the water. They started wading back up to the bank and proceeded to the trailer for the ride back. Out of the corner of my eye I spotted a figure diving into the river. As he made his way out into the water where the current was quicker, I shouted "No!" I began unlacing my boots to go after him. When I looked up again, he had too much of a lead. A clamor broke out among the other prisoners. I didn't know what they were saying. Harry yelled for him to come back and waved while shouting "Dien cai dao! Dien cai dao!" meaning "You're crazy." Now in my stocking feet, I picked up my rifle. The ROKs ran over to see what the trouble was. Harry pointed to the escaped prisoner in the water. I shouldered my M-16 and commenced firing single shots at the fleeing man.

He was about 50 yards out in the river. The ROKs started firing too. The M-1s made loud booms, canon like. He swam under water and came up for air while the current swept him downstream. I aimed and waited for him to come up for air. When he did, I fired a short volley on semi-automatic and missed. He dove back under and then came back up high out of the water, arms outstretched. His face and chest were facing us. I fired again, as did the ROKs. After I pulled the trigger, I saw a cloud of red spray burst out behind his head. He sank and never came up. We quit our firing, and two Vietnamese fishermen in a boat paddled out to where he had gone under. Finally, drifting downstream a short distance, they pulled his body to the surface and into the boat. Harry was watching the other prisoners. Their eyes were solemn as they looked straight out toward their comrade's body in the boat. They waited silently.

Harry called into headquarters on the jeep's radio and explained what happened. He was informed that a truck would be dispatched to pick up the body and then for us to return to camp. Once the fishermen arrived ashore, people gathered around the dead man. A blue cast had begun to settle into the waxy white corpse, a grimace on his face, eyes squinched shut and a small bloody hole in his forehead. I could not make myself look at the back of his head. Just below his right thumb was a bullet hole.

Later, I wondered what his last seconds of life were like. Maybe after he was wounded in the hand, he realized he could not escape. Perhaps that's why he turned toward us and sprang chest high out of the water with arms outstretched, to give himself up. God! I had to quit thinking about it, or his image would haunt my dreams for a lifetime.

During the dire trip back to the POW compound, none of our seven captives spoke or looked at us. I sensed contempt in their eyes and a certain sadness and reverence for the loss of their comrade. He was a rice farmer probably just trying to make his way back home to his once thriving valley.

After we delivered them, I wanted to retreat to the tent, have a cold beer, smoke pot, share the story. I was young and not quite a soldier. I didn't yet realize the implications of killing an unarmed, defenseless man, of taking a life. For several nights my heart and mind tossed in anguish. It all happened too fast. I had felt something in that instant. Something I had not felt since first shooting a rabbit during my youth and having it die in my hand. Something I had hoped to never experience again, never see or feel again.

Frijole Beach, California: 1977

At Frijole Beach seagulls hovered in the balmy draft and searched the waves. Their winded tufts of feathers matched the whitecaps. My pal Gurney steered the tan Volkswagen van into the parking lot. He cut the engine, reached into his shoulder bag and pulled out a small prescription vial. He dispensed two capsules of MDA and reached one to me. We uncapped them, poured the white powder into our beer bottles and headed down to the surf. After listening to the breakers and feeling the warm October air, we moseyed over past the beach, to a berth of black lava rock, fissured by millennia of weather and waves. The tide was ebbing, leaving small pools of water in the bowled fissures. We sat down. Gulls shrieked and strutted across the sand. The air was rich with salt. Gurney turned on his portable cassette recorder and began recording our conversation as an audio letter to our Army friend serving in Germany.

On that almost cloudless day, as the MDA seeped in, we chatted. Eventually, I spoke about Vietnam, the first time I'd ever been able to talk about it though I had returned home a decade earlier. Finally, I told Gurney of a recurring dream regarding an incident at the An Lao River. I described a POW, a peasant, a rice farmer. He attempted to escape, swimming down the river. I had to shoot him.

When I finished my story, I looked down into a small pool of water, in the dark lava in front of us. There was a baby octopus, trapped, not much bigger than my thumb. The delicate orange creature was struggling, its tiny tentacles reaching to find a way out of the enclosed pool of salt water.

Then Gurney spoke to me.

"You said something very interesting, Jack. You mentioned an image, 'a cloud of red,' after you shot him."

I thought hard about that, not realizing I had said it that way, having been caught up in the moment of the nightmare. We talked on. The incident in Vietnam had lived in my disturbed dreams and thoughts for ten years. The MDA had had an effect I had never experienced. It opened me up, lightening my heart. It heightened my empathy and made it easier for me to talk. But, more importantly, a close friend had listened and responded to my story, ultimately freeing me to later write the song "Cloud of Red" and sing about the event in the months to come in my regular music and storytelling performances.

As the sun sank lower, our time at Frijole Beach was drawing to a close. Gurney clicked off the recorder. I reached down and gently scooped up the little orange octopus into my palm. I walked out into the receding tide and returned it to the sea.

Excerpted from a memoir-in-progress, *Scrap Iron*.

Catherine Hamrick

My Father on D-Day and Mountain Shade

They said the LST could ride higher
in the water when landing in trim,

and on a stomach-churning morning,
she hit the beach slope; the bow door fell,

disgorging jeeps and tanks and finally us;
it was gray all around—the water, the sky,

the ships, as far as I could see, the one time
I looked back, and then only forward.

They made movies of our memories,
of what they thought they were:

German mortar and exploding artillery,
the strewn wreckage of flipped, ripped jeeps,

of wire, of bodies, whole, some with faces yet,
of twitching pieces, arms here and legs flung there,

of middle parts oozing guts—the sea foams,
so does blood. Then my hands did the thinking,

and doing, on semi-automatic,
what the doctor ordered: stanch bleeding,

apply dressings, sprinkle sulfa powder,
(the lone wound antiseptic) and dwindle

the morphine— on who has the best chance;
the hands became the machine that patched

the broken living, passing them to other hands
that stretchered them up the ramp.

I paused. Once. At the strangeness of it all.
Why Omaha? A city in a golden-prairie ocean.

Why Utah? A landlocked state with a salt lake.
But this Omaha, this Utah, opened to a dead sea,

where boys stepped to rock bottom
off Higgins boats, murdered by their gear.

I saw, in a blind moment,
the north Georgia mountain shade—

and tulip poplars growing straight,
reliably, their futures in coffins.

"Their wood is best," said Lem Moss, maker
of final boxes, "fast growing and long-lived."

When did coffins become caskets?
"Jewelry is for caskets," said my mother,

midwife and layer out of the dead,
giving up a bed sheet to line

somebody else's final sleep, east-facing,
because that was the way it was always done;

she held them at their beginning,
and at their end—I was the lucky one,

finally home, for that long in between
when she held me in the mountain shade

one more time, many times over:
the boy, the man, the graying son.

Flavian Mark Lupinetti

Mingo County, 1921

Dory Clef survived the Great War.
Survived bullets, bayonets, and gas.
Survived generals, kings, and presidents.
Survived the perfidy of bankers who
placed their bets on who would win
and egged on America's involvement as a hedge.
Once back home, these mountains felt impregnable
to Dory, the ultimate defense against
an occupying force.
Dory Clef could not have known
that Mingo County already stood occupied,
every tree and creek and lump of coal
in the clench of empire's fist.
The owners of the mines took
exception to a union,
an existential threat against their empire.
They never put a foot in West Virginia,
yet their fingers pulled the trigger of the gun
that the Pinkerton merely carried,
violating Dory's rib cage,
corrupting Dory's lung.

> Let us now pause to ponder
> what it means to gargle,
> the stimulus and response
> that follow pulmonary trauma.
> To gargle, an act of pure volition,
> a product of paired urges in opposition:
> one, a need to clear the airway;

two, the horror at propelling
one's own blood onto muddy ground,
the way that Dory Clef commenced
to gargle away the remaining hours of his life.

Noah Davis

God Came to Me

God lifted her doe head and offered
me her fur throat.

From her nose blood pumped lung-rhythm,
fountained by my bullet
aimed too far back.

I cut God's throat,
and her warmth melted the snow.

I eat God each day and pray
in the way she taught me
to pray: catching her breath in my lungs.

Byron Hoot

Of That Nature

I am a pagan born into
a preacher's home. When
I learned to pray, I
offered prayers up and out,
into the sky, into the woods
thinking a prayer here or there
no problem, the praying
the important thing releasing
what was inside, opening
to what would come, brushing
aside the words that wanted
to be said in answer.
Prayers to the sky,
prayers to the woods,
prayers coming from deep
inside, rising, emptying
me, making room for
answers to arrive—
so I learned to pray easily
here and there, answers
coming likewise

Julie Byrne
Seeing Eye God

Ceramic Sculpture
Original photograph credit: Tessa Berg (Starling Studio)

Chiquita Mullins Lee

Seeing Eye God

Seeing Eye God,
birthing I grow
walking I stand
standing I see.
Seeing I God

Yesterday's mud
flavored my mood
sun—my foe,
clay—my food.
Stumbling I stand.
Running I slide.
Wagging I tail.
Seeing I God.

I'm my best twin
I grew my friend.
Daily, I trod.
Seeing, eye God.

John C. Mannone

Antietam Creek

Algonquian for swift water
that flows to the Potomac
on fire with that smell
of memory—black powder
burning its sulfur. It's a place
where the grass is silvery,
cool, lush with chokeberry
at wood's edge. By the bridge,
in the meadow, black-eyed
Susans collage with lavender
butterflies lilting in the wind—
a hush of wings—flower to flower
carpeting the rich brown soil.
But any smiles are evanescent.
Grass tufts splay from seams
in limestone, conceal
the pockmarks, the blur
in my eyes from hot bullet
stings from the past. Shadows
of mayapples cannot hide
the scent, or blood that once
flowed like water over flat shale
and lead slugs, smooth or jagged
with that heart-shaped glitter
of gray and blue under the sear
of a late-afternoon September sun.

Roy Bentley

First Haircut

The Confederate flag
unfurls from the antenna
of my father's '32 Ford Coupe
replica—a fiberglass body with a rumble
seat on a '72 Mustang chassis: 302 V-8 with
an automatic and standard brakes and nothing
like power steering, a recipe for disaster. But
his Old Kentucky Homeplace is in the Ford,

and this morning he wants to take my new son
Matt, his first grandchild, to the Shear Shoppe
for a first haircut. We all have our demons.
Most of mine have to do with having stopped
loving my father. I'm holding my 8-month-old
when my pops says he'd like to bring his Leica.
Says it as if there's nothing else to say. The sun-
up-gold Ford is idling, flag flapping. Nevertheless,

I'm recalling my professor, Horace Coleman, a poet
who once christened Black America the engine under
the hood of Thomas Jefferson's America. I know my
father; however, I'm learning what it takes to get him
to lose the Confederate flag. It's quiet. Then he laughs.
I see Horace, a veteran of the one war that never ends,
the contest not to be bullied into living untruthfully or
without honor: Horace is nodding, saying *I told you so.*

Mother waves from the picture window of their house.
Maybe it's the beauty and hope of having a new son, but
I tell him *No way* and wait until he grabs the cloth fabric
and rides it up the antenna. Off. A nimbus of bottle flies
is brushed from the fender by his motions. He's pissed
as he folds the flag. He says for me to put it in the glove
box. I'm holding Matt, but he tries to hand it off to me.
I give him a look and he says to get in the damn car.

Lisa Parker

Republic: 2017-2020

> *The sound we do not hear lifts the gulls off the water.*
> —From Ilya Kaminsky's "Town," *Deaf Republic*

What ear hears the dog bark a warning from yard
or woods, but not the executioner's gun?

The deaf—who we call *impaired*—know
not to turn away, know
self-preservation and mercy aren't the kissing cousins
the church would say they are, the Christ-vanished clucking
of eye-averters to children in cages, stuffing the benches full
of the like-minded, gladhanding the near hysteria
of political pulpits, covet robes and verdicts in exchange
for children in tin foil blankets, toddlers
snatched past the margin of record, disappeared,
or washed up
face down
on the banks and shores.
The deaf know copper-laced air to be red
without looking.
Do not turn away.
Note the executioner when he comes
in his tie and lapel-pin patriotism.
Note which direction the gun is pointed, my friends.
As the story goes, if the townspeople had run at him
at once, all together, no shot would've been fired,
nothing spilled to pavement or detention floors, the gulls
would still sleep on pier poles
in air unbroken.

Steven T. Licardi

Morphology

The stink of it lingers everywhere.

To a fish, is the ocean
salty?
Does it smell like death?
Is it the flavor of
anything at all?

Such is the thievery of White Supremacy.
A drowning that makes me, a man, forget
that I have gills.
Stands like a desecration—
a monument to remind itself
of its own forgetting.

It looks—well,
it looks like me.
Tastes like how my tongue tastes
or the way my eyes look.

Maybe,
White Supremacy *is* me.
A monument meant to be
dismantled.
Co-opted anxiety. Guilt
that disguises itself as culpability.

I thought
I washed it out from the corners
of my smile. Bleached it away
from between my teeth.

I thought I scrubbed it clean
from my slick skin,
but even flesh can be colonized.
Like scabies or botflies.
School never taught me that
imperialism can fly.

Do birds know what the sky
feels like?
The texture of air as it passes
through their wings?

Ducks never chew their food
before swallowing.

Where I come from
we call that
choking.

Carson Colenbaugh

Fear of Burning

Holding the line on Crooked Creek,
USFS-743C covered in gravel soot, my careless drips
   of diesel and little flames,
The crew boys downroad with chainsaw tearing through
   the snag of some Virginia pine—
We call this fuel reduction, we call this oak regen.

Centuries past was for chestnut,
Open the greenwood into forage for deer (this is food,
   this is company), get berries—get acorns—
Set a good blaze and bring back the grass.

Now it's in the hands of the yellowshirts,
I eat apples and nibble on wintergreen, the vehicles and fat
   tires pounding on the ground the industrial drumbeat;
No room for rabbit, the inner wounds of yellow pines mark
   the scorching earth saying
"I was burned before and I'll burn again."
All this before the torching of villages and older yet
   than Smokey Bear.

4:28 p.m. and watching the last trees cinder on the floor,
Burning the small dead branches in a warm pile while some
   guy talks about caring for a longnose brown bat—
*"Oh she made it a nice little bed on the ground and stepped
   on its head when she reached for her lunch."*
Not knowing the blood of giants, the tradition of stone,
   the cost of stealing fire.

Victor Depta

Bear Branch Farm

They're not listening to themselves, and I probably wouldn't be
    able to stand it, to tell you the truth, if I weren't stoned, the
    kind where you can't lift a finger for the THC and don't
    want to even if you could, like levitating in chains from a
    lounge chair among my kin—he may be worthless (I know
    what they say) but he wouldn't harm a flea, mostly
    because he don't have the wherewithal to find one on his
    neck

the old folks at the edge of dark, chattering on the porch about some
    relative as far back as Lucy and that Turkana boy—
    whatever happened to those children, anyhow?—I mean
    we suffer and there's nothing we can do about it, like the
    kids in the yard with their toys from the Dollar Tree—I
    don't mind spending a few bucks—a foam-rubber football,
    a Frisbee and Styrofoam airplanes, though it's evening
    enough that the bats could carry them off

I mean I love my grandpa and grandma, but they've been at it all
    day, and so have my aunts and uncles—now Hank, stop
    spitting in the yard, people will think you're trash—and
    bless it, William, stop eating so fast, you ain't no hog, and
    besides, you'll get the hiccups—and Sally Jean, you're
    dripping watermelon on your belly, the juice'll draw
    wasps and you're ruining your blouse—and Freddy, don't
    ever cut toward yourself with a knife

God. Hasn't my family ever heard of Pink Floyd telling them to
        leave them kids alone?—yes, when a dog dies it goes to
        heaven—you all wear them ballcaps, if you don't,
        the deer flies will eat you up—my god, Freddie,
        don't you know that's poison ivy?—when they're
        older, when they're teenagers, they'll get as far away
        as possible from all those cautions—they'll be free to
        injure themselves however they like

but not now, not with darkness coming on, they play close
        to the porch, ignoring as best they can their elders'
        admonitions—god bless it, Hank, you threw that
        Frisbee in the creek on purpose, those rocks are slick
        and you'll break your neck—and William, that
        airplane will end up on the roof and you won't have
        one—and Sally Jean, you're tearing that baby doll's
        arms clear off its body, so stop it!—lord, you
        children, it's a miracle we all aren't nuts

it's a miracle sure enough, and I could drink me a beer, a
        six-pack of Rolling Rock—no, you can't sacrifice
        those crawdads in the fire, people don't sacrifice any
        more, so you take that jar and pour them back in the
        creek—and mercy god, you all stop stumbling around
        the fire—and yes, I'm getting the stuff for the s'mores

and there we are, with a fire in the dark, with the orange
        flames and the sparks rising to the stars—if you
        could see them beyond the glare and your shins
        getting scorched—with lightning bugs and injury
        and pain and death near us everywhere, the place
        where love's dear irritating cries cry out, *be careful!*
        be careful! be careful!

64

Randel McCraw Helms

Me and My Baby Brother Has Some of the Good Stuff

Now this time I'm nearbout too old for whuppin,
But by God I get a goodun anyhow.
I'm fourteen, and I know Daddy has him a still
Out in the woods somewhere. Then one day I find
A big jug of his good stuff hid under the hay
In the corn crib. Now my baby brother Chase
He's four, and I think it'd be fun to teach him
How to drink like a man, and I'll have me some too.
This was not long before supper. Them days,
We don't have us but the one old rooster,
And Mama needs him for topping the hens,
So Daddy he ain't killed us no chickens lately.
It's the end of winter, and hog meat's gone.
It's Sunday, and we don't have us no meat
At all, just a cold pone and some taters
And a few of them hen fruits, which I never
Much cared for, you don't get you no good food
Out of no chicken's ass. Mama has done told me
About our piss pore supper, so I think I'll get
Chase, now he's good and drunk, to jump on Daddy
About this, and I teach him what to say.
So Chase, he struts into the kitchen, and his tongue
Is real thick from all that good shine, and he says, "Cleve,
By God you can kill a damn hen or leave home, one."

You see why I can't avoid no whuppin this time.

65

Scott T. Hutchinson

Finding

a naked boy in your teenaged daughter's closet:
you'd heard some strange bumping, dressed
to investigate, asked the parental *everything okay?*
and heard just enough clothes hanger jangle
to open that door. You call through the wall *Honey,*
would you come in here and take a look at this?
Your daughter jabbers something incensed
and despairing, but you're looking at the boy:
covering, maybe a few months past hairless,
and his eyes and open mouth scream
in the abject silence of mortal fear.
A half turn to the window produces
open panes, and poking your head out
you see your own aluminum ladder, the one
usually collapsed and leaning against the side—
now opened to full length, up to your daughter's
second story window. But there are two copies
of *Romeo & Juliet* lying on the floor, two
open bookbags. The adults back out, invite
two for hot chocolate downstairs
as soon as they're ready.

Owen Cramer

Thirteen Ways for
Staying Happily Married
to an Appalachian Woman
When You Are Not Appalachian

So, flatlander, you married an Appalachian woman. Maybe you are from Chicago or New York or someplace like that, but you married her anyway. Of all the mountains in all the countries, you married her. Now you have to make it work and this can help. You will find no basic stuff here like how to pronounce Appalachia or how you should never mention Uncle Jed, Ellie May or Aunt Bea, even if she has an Aunt Bea. This is advanced degree stuff—like what to say (or do) in certain circumstances—and when not to say (or do) anything at all. They are both important but for God's sake do not get them mixed up.

1. Be careful when she says "*I Reckon.*" It means she disagrees with you. If you ask her a question like "*Hey, honey how about this paint color or that brand of soap?*" and she says "*I reckon,*" then you reply "*I-don't-like-it.*" You do that and everything will be fine, I reckon.

2. She is not from a city or a town. She is from a <u>county</u>. And when someone mentions a nearby county, you need to say "*Well, I hear people from that county aren't any good.*"

3. A man and his Appalachian woman are one. A man and his Appalachian woman and her family are one,

too. You married the whole fam damily. Get used to it. And, if she says to someone, *"Who are you to me?"*—don't say anything. It's OK. She is not starting a feud. She is just trying to understand the family relationship.

4. The cornbread doesn't have any sugar in it. Don't say anything, don't mention it. Just eat it. Shush.

5. Soup beans don't come with soup. Don't say anything about that either. Speaking of beans, I hope you like green beans, half runners, shucky beans, whatever. Just don't get them confused. If you don't know your beans, then don't open your piehole.

6. It's pronounced "Paah-hole."

7. That unsweet cornbread and the soup beans without soup? It's dinner. Sorry, it's not dinner. It's supper. And when she says the family will be joining us for supper tonight, don't ask which ones. It doesn't matter anyway. Just say *"I sure hope they leave me some soup beans and cornbread"* and then just shut up and eat.

8. Get-your-shoes-off-the-quilt.

9. If you ever *"go back"* for a funeral that requires going to the cemetery, rent a four-wheel drive truck. Also, get directions before you go. You can't ask for directions from a stranger because the name of the cemetery changes based on family relationships. That's why people ask questions like *"who are you to me?"* – so they can find the damn cemetery.

10. She has a cast iron pan. Don't ever use it, don't touch it and never put it in the dishwasher.

11. Someday, you might buy a house and want to redo-the-landscape-together. Don't do it. You will start talking about putting in a nice Bradford pear here and a weeping cherry there—and she will spend the rest of the marriage talking about how you wanted to plant fruit trees that don't have any fruit. Your wife only wants to grow two things in the yard: things to eat and things to take to the cemetery. Do it her way. Your yard won't look like the neighbor's, but you'll be happier.

12. Colleges outside your wife's home state might have basketball teams. I forget. You forget, too. And for God's sake, if your alma mater plays your wife's basketball team, do not watch the game with her cousins.

13. You remember her cousins from the wedding. They took you aside to say they would "*kill-you-dead*" if you ever hurt your new wife. The cousins are serious about that "*kill-you-dead*" stuff but it will be OK. Just keep on eating your cornbread, finding your own way to the cemetery and talking smack about the people in the next county and they won't hurt you. I reckon. The cousins might even come in handy someday unless you do something stupid…like put a cast-iron pan in the dishwasher.

Jimmy Long

Boundaries

One night before we moved to the country,
one of the neighbor sisters was "it" and I hid so well
in the prayerful maple boughs, I must have darkened
to bark. I was a strange and camouflaged being then,
hugging the rough embroidery to my face as I waited
with clenched eyes to feel a girl's fingers through my shirt.
I think now it was like the moment before the first
time I was touched as a man, when life's electricity rocketed
back to my body, its ground. But I never felt her
sweet tingle outside my imagination. Instead of grinning me
she found my uncle after six or seven Old Milwaukees
spraying the moonlight clover, sealing me in the territory
of solitude. After that, both stayed on their side of the invisible
line which divided our yards. But O how I wanted a sister, to be
groomed and smoothed by an older girl's touch. The boys
I knew were so cruel. We moved to the farmhouse where
all I could hear sometimes was a brook fizzing
like an empty stomach. I remember being shocked
to learn our fathers had sunk iron pins in the earth
to mark the boundaries of our land, that boundaries could be
treasures so precious we had to bury them down.

Jessica Cory

Image of My Estranged Grandfather
at 94

Pecks of tomatoes. 27 blue
   ribbons. 3 cans of Pabst
water the sandy throat

parched from sprinkled
   sunlight & Sevin dust.
Darkened fingertips lava-

soap scrubbed pink as cherry
   blossoms. His long
love affair with the land, that bond

stronger than the one with his own kin.

Jane Ann Fuller

A Kind of Grief

Dear D,

See the sycamores' bony arms reaching up
like old men dying?
What do they want from us?
What *could* they want?

I've been driving the creek down Pleasant Valley
to the corner of Star Route.
I've been listening,
really listening.

I know you forgive your father, but
I don't know if we can share grief
since like a bird,
it seems indivisible.

You didn't know looking at this piece of sky
would be a look at you,
lone goose crying for its flock long gone
its family long, long gone.

But you must have known I'd miss him
since it's not a body I hold, but memory
like a dog squatting to pee on my perennials,
the flowers just standing there
saying nothing.

There's a knot on my neck that runs down the shoulder blade.
This could be what it feels like to have a wing
broken. Think *water, sky. Dark bird.*

A bald eagle flew above our car yesterday as we drove
    toward the lake.
It zoomed overhead like a *deux ex machina.*
We talked about the sighting for days. White gliding into white.
The superior bird freed like a dog from a kill kennel
we would take home and feed scraps,
let nap on our hearth like on an oversized pillow.

Where does that leave us?
We no longer belong
to sky or water. Our bones separate
from themselves. Is that what they want us to know?

If I were a bird, I am sure,
my right wing would be broken,
but I am no bird, and my bones are so heavy
I sink when I try to float.

Deni Naffziger

Last Lesson

Dear J,

Do you remember
when he tipped you back,
held your head
in the cup of his hand—
your arms wide,
eyes fixed
on seabirds
and swallows?
Now he has let go
and you are prepared
as he intended
for the riptide that pulls you
to the ocean floor
like a star fish caught
between gravity
and weightlessness. The body
knows its pharyngeal gills
trade water for remembrance.
You will breathe like this
for weeks or months
or longer
and when you return
waves of grief will find you
making your mother's bed.
Drop everything since nothing
can fight the force
of water.

Ask rocks and rivers
how many tears
it took to shape
the shore.

Joanne Greenway

The Water Witch

> *Martin Luther condemned divination an act of*
> *heresy, but St. Theresa of Avila built her*
> *convent where a dowser had found water.*

Sam Horn churned up a cloud of dust,
his old beater lurching up the dirt lane.
A small crowd had gathered, eager to see
if a man could find water with a stick.

Along for the ride, a trunk-load of dowsing rods:
peach, willow and hazel-wood. For this job,
he chose the hazel-wood. My father had
rarely drilled a dry hole. If he was skeptical,
he was curious, too—it was a drought year.

Over his short-sleeved shirt, Sam wore
a catcher's chest protector. As he paced
the property, my brother Bo and I trailed
him until he stopped short and lurched
wildly, staggering to keep his feet—
engaged in a tug-of-war with a demon.

The forked branch then suddenly jerked
ground-ward. *Plant the stake right there,*
at the tip o' my foot, he instructed Bo.
Eyes closed, face tilted skyward, the twig
tapped out on his padded chest how deep
the water lay. The unforgiving July sun
beat down; his shirt darkened with sweat.

This spectacle repeated several times.
Was he a charlatan or was there some
spiritual connection between man and
element? Scientists insist the rods'
movement is an "ideomotor response,"
not due to some hidden agent. No more
believable than alchemy or astrology.

Bo has been a driller—and a water witch—
for over sixty years. Instead of a branch,
he uses two bent brass rods. When he walks
over a vein, he swears the rods move, outward.

My brother is a Pisces—he always finds water.

Kari Gunter-Seymour

Badasses

Sunday afternoon. Taylor Swift's latest nonsense
caterwauls the radio, a third-string agitation,
compared to my son trying to bootlick his daughter
into jumping in our pond off the high dive,
nine feet up a steep-planked ladder.

A pinch of a girl, she just this week turned six
and I wonder where that rascal in him comes from.
I blame his father, long gone and good riddance.
My true husband, a gem, who knows me all too well,
taps his sandaled foot against my pinky-toe,
slightly shakes his head, because my granddaughter
just cold-shouldered her daddy, ran to fetch
her fishing pole instead.

Though I don't want it, those twelve soccer boys,
clear the other side of the world, are on my mind.
Trapped miles inside a cave, tides rising, huddled
and hungry, licking water drops from crusty walls.
Last week, Navy SEALs rose from the depths
like apparitions, brought pep talks, promises,
concocting on the fly, ways those boys, who don't
even know how to swim, can strap on a face mask,
practice a few strokes, MacGyver their way free.

We cool ourselves in the water, ride four-wheelers,
reach for icy Coca-Colas, popsicles, slices of melon.
We're fixing to wind down when breaking
news blasts the radio. *Christ almighty,*

four of those boys made it out, others
not far behind, SEALs at their backs, urging.

Soon after, my wily son afloat below the dive,
that plucky grandbaby of mine sets down her pole,
climbs the ladder, leaps like a fish-nymph,
hoots as she breaks the surface.

Marc Harshman

What I've Seen

For thus hath the Lord said unto me,
Go, set a watchman, let him declare what he seeth.
—*King James Version*, Isaiah 21:6

1

Not what's expected
    but what hides out of sight
    glorious and dark, pregnant, unknown.

The overnight umbrella opened up
    from fragile mycelium
    offers itself to the hungry light.

The oriole loudly whistling overhead
    in the dense canopy of summer
    gives away nothing but himself.

The wriggle in the coppery leaves below
    the leaning gravity of dripping sandstone cliffs:
        a rattlesnake carrying poison enough
        for me and for you, enough
        from which we might learn to strike.

The legacy of Mother Jones in her "dangerous fields,"
    shot at and carried on a miner's back
    up from the shadows to save the idea
    might liberate the future, out of sight now
    but saved quick, sharp, and ready.

The nurse and doctor down along the river,
        nosing out the homeless camps,
        dispensing without applause
        bandages, pills, Narcan, the gift
        of listening however long
        into the small hours.
In the shadows of those small hours the names
        whispering:
                PurduePharma, Cardinal Health,
                McKesson, Americsource....

                        2

As for the valley fill, fly ash, the MCHM,
        the fracker's sandy, chemical-laced brine,
        the floods, rock falls, earthquakes,
        contamination, black lung, cancers,
        well, there are other names:
        Williams, Chesapeake, Halliburton,
        Exxon and Peabody, Arch, Consol,
        Murray, Baker Hughes, Dow-Dupont,
        IEI, MarkWest, Freedom Industries . . .
        names, so many names.

Names that call to mind other names, other places:
        Buffalo Creek, Kayford Mountain,
        Larry Gibson, Tug River, Judy Bonds,
        Brookside, South Parkersburg, Blair,
        Vera Scroggins, Elk River, Maria Gunnoe,
        more losses than victories in these battles
        but as long as their memories
        entangle our own, there's kindling.

3

The spectral moon slips over the beech grove,
      traces of reflected light
      ignite the pale trunks, set fire, loose
      the testimonies.

String the sweet-bitter catgut of ourselves
      onto the dark fiddles, bow us onward
      in the cortege that ends in dance
      and free us from every sonofabitch
      absentee landlord and corporate puppet-master
      whose will was never our own.

Clyde Kessler

Jackie Betkin Quits Fiddling

So I ease back from here to Woolwine
through the woods, cautioned home.
Old frog works loose from the fiddle bow,
and I dream how that happens, how I failed,
and now it's a real frog half-jumped from ebony,
chirping for rain. My cousins swear my whiskey
makes me see things, makes tadpoles swim
through fog, makes a spring branch whicker
with toads. I know how to ruin a fiddle, they say,
because when I tune up, wild cats run, dogs growl,
and a whole flock of owls hoots the sun backwards.
Ghosts shinny through the barn planks, then set fire
to themselves. They hold their skulls above the sky
trying to escape. So I sneak home, and stop fiddling,
like sliding away, and fingering a million thorns.

Melissa Helton

Sometimes the Dead

Sometimes the dead don't stay dead, rising
on anniversaries to trail their acrid fingers
through the potato salad. Sometimes the dead
appear as a trace of citrus and sandalwood
while you contemplate a lightning-struck oak
in Tennessee. Sometimes the dead were never
even born, little acorns that couldn't become
lightning-struck oaks. Sometimes the dead are merciful
in their absence, leaving spaces between air molecules
empty. Sometimes the dead are abandoned, faded
sepia photographs and etched tintypes in a cardboard box
on the antique store shelf. Sometimes the dead do not
know they are dead and they stomp around, still living
their lives in the dark synapses of a brain. Sometimes
the dead know they are dead, as they are pulled apart
by wind like wood smoke in the valley. Sometimes
the dead are waiting. Sometimes the dead won't wake up.

Chrissie Anderson Peters

The Witness

The first time I communicated with the dead, it was my great-grandmother, Granny Vance, and I was in first grade. I had spent nearly every day of my young life in Granny's presence. She had been sick for some time. I recall it was late May, one of those days when it was quite warm outside, and warmer inside as my grandparents had no central air in their white doublewide in 1978. My cousin Melenia and her parents were visiting. The doctors had told the family to come in because Granny was not long for this world. Before she got so bad, a few weeks earlier, our moms, Granny's granddaughters, had snuck us to just outside her room at the hospital, by taking us up the fire escape of the hospital. Back then, people kept visiting hours. And children under the age of twelve were not permitted in hospital rooms. Period.

My Aunt Susan, Mom's younger sister, had the task of taking care of Melenia and me, Melenia being almost exactly a year younger than me. She had brought us back to Mamaw and Papaw's house earlier that day and we played together, as cousins do. As the evening wore on, Melenia went to bed in the middle bedroom, where she was staying with her parents on their visit. My own mother and Mamaw's sister Betty would take the night shift with Granny, while other family members waited at the hospital in the waiting room. She was, for all intents and purposes, in a coma, and really did not know who was or was not with her.

I fell asleep in a pair of shorts and a t-shirt on the old brown Naugahyde couch in the living room

85

before bedtime, watching television. Something big was happening; I understood that much. I knew that Granny had been sick for a long time. Being an only child who was raised as much by Mamaw and Papaw as by Mom, I had been to my fair share of funerals already, folks we had gone to church with, family members, and older family friends. I understood the rituals of death, even if not the actual dying.

Suddenly, as I slept, I could see Granny Vance's face. She was sitting in front of me, but it was as though a fine mist surrounded her. I pushed and pulled and twisted hard, trying to get away from her. Her hair was down, and it scared me. Granny never wore her hair down and I knew that something was wrong. She called me by name, then said, "Listen to me, child, there's no use in you fighting Granny like that. I have some things to tell you, things that you need to hear. So you just lay still and listen to me. Listen now, hush!" And she smiled at me tenderly.

I immediately calmed down and began listening. "In your lifetime, many things will happen," she told me. "And there are other things that you are not to do." Then she presented me with a list of each. To say that I remember either list completely these forty-some years later would be a lie, but growing up, there have been times when my decisions of whether or not to do something or to go somewhere were guided by a sort of "knowledge" that I firmly believe came from somewhere else, someone else, who was looking out for me, as I've always believed that she was my guardian angel and was doing just that. I have achieved certain things that I know for certain were on that list, the moment that they happened, remembering her voice telling me that I would do them. The lists seemed to go on forever, and I grew tired of listening; I just wanted to wake up. Granny looked at me sternly. "You can't wake up until I finish talking to you. There's more you need to know." She went on. "People around you will be very sad. They shouldn't be. And I don't want you to be, either. I'm going to heaven and I won't have to be sick anymore. So when everyone else is crying, you hug them and tell them that Granny's watching them, and they better start smiling again!" She leaned in through the mist and kissed me on the forehead. "Child, I love you so very much. And any time you need me, I will be right here for you. Even though I'm dead, I promise I'll still be right here." She folded her arms around me and kissed me once more, and as she pulled away, she said quietly, "You can wake up now, honey. Granny's dead."

At that moment, the phone rang, and I bolted upright on the couch, drenched in sweat. I could hear my mother's voice on the other end saying that Granny had just passed away, that she would be home in a little while. When she got home, she took me in the back bedroom to begin explaining to me that Granny had died. I calmly responded, "I know. She told me." When my mother asked what I meant, I told her about Granny telling me that she was dying. Mom seemed panicked to hear me talk so matter-of-factly about my experience. But it was every bit as real as anything else I have ever encountered in my life.

For the next nearly-two years, I saw and spoke with Granny Vance almost daily. We walked and talked together around the farm where I lived. No one else saw her. No one else heard her. But I witnessed her on many occasions. Just before the end of 1980, I dreamed one night that she came to our door. Again, her hair was down, and she called out my name from the door. I went to the door to see what she needed. She told me that it was time for her to "go on," but she did not want me to think that I had imagined any of what we had shared. So, she was leaving me a friend to remind me of her after she was not beside me every day. And in the dream, she bent down, and a shadow moved in front of the door and I looked up to see her no more.

On New Year's Eve, my grandparents, and my cousin Melenia and her parents, were at our house to bring in the new year. I heard the screen door bang open and looked up, thinking I saw someone on the porch. When I got to the door, a shadow moved in front of the door, and when I looked down, there was a little puppy dog standing in the cold. He looked just like the dog from the Benji movies from the 70s. Benji stayed with us as an outside dog for quite some time. I always believed that he was Granny's way of helping me transition so that she could go to be in heaven full-time, but I never doubted that she was still looking out for me from up there. I had, after all, witnessed her promises and prophesies firsthand.

Jane Hicks

Buick Reverie

I saw my mother's car today—
a sand-colored Buick that drove and rode like a boat,
an old folks car, all leather, all automatic, full chrome.
Her hope to drive again stillborn in ICU after the crash that
left her unconscious for days. Reflexes too slow for traffic,
we cruised the parking lots of closed stores
until she realized her worst truth. Mini-strokes,
A-fib and medications wrecked her independence.

I piloted that craft four or five times a week
to doctor after doctor, the grocery, unending
Walmart trips where she still raced the aisles
in her motored cart, and on her penultimate day,
I struggled her chair from the car into the heart center
where they attached monitors that sent an ambulance
when she stroked out the next day.

The man who owns the Buick lives across the ridge—
five miles of curvy country roads wind between.
Once a mechanic, he bought it without haggling.
declared that engine model a miracle
of longevity. The exchange paid the legal fee
to settle her estate, finalized a life.

I followed and remembered as we navigated
the back roads toward the highway.
At the intersection, we turned opposite ways,
the taillights flashed and her car sailed away.

Ali Hintz

winter light like a dentist's office and I'm reading Ross Gay

I hear a knock
put on a t-shirt
unlock the door
open to a cardboard box
   treasure
lay it on the old pine floor
pull a knife
from the overstrewn coffee table
   slice
the piece of tape
sideways lengthwise sideways
   seethrough bag of pearls
mixed lot
rice blue knotted
   pearls
I lay them out neat
on the floor I
pick up a strand and
push it to my neck
run my callouses over
their bumps and I
thank the oysters
for their lives and the intrusion
of sand they swallowed and
calcified to protect their tender
organs shucked from shell
from pearl I hope
their shells sank

to the bottom of the sea
to be pushed back into rock
and three billion years from you, dear reader,
an alien new being will take
your fossilized shell
in their hand
in the middle of
a mountain valley
filled with alien soybeans
and put you up
to their ear to hear
the sea

Timothy Dodd

The Cardinal, Through West Virginia

Out the Amtrak window, so much
          floats by: wintry wave in tree spire
and rolling hills under a foggy grey
          heaven, then pastures with small herds
of cattle, homestead set in the corner
          and Mail Pouch-sided barns balancing
the farm; you can't miss the ferroalloy
          plants in the foothills either, or a gorge
filled with green water, square boulders
          chiseled and polished on its banks.
Bear, eagle, and deer claw and soar,
          scampering over these tracks; ghost
towns and creeks gurgle, spin tales.
          The burst of image, retina-jump, flare,

then another, is an upheaval of time,
          these minutes more than many lifetimes,
a dazzle of the land and moments
          of man etched upon it; carried in slow
defense, the animals chewing, prodding,
          hiding, perhaps dizzier from our design.
Behind glass, in a reclining seat drinking
          gin and iced espresso, our earth moves
at a rate our calculations can't measure;
          forward, forward, shooting through it all
—but in reverse, the result isn't the same:
          to race back into a presence of the past
would fill our bay with weary phantoms,
          a blurry begging for us to grant them life.

Rita Coleman

My Mother's Geography

Holy water, poised until snail darters are safe, gushes
over watermelon patches, cornfields, pastureland, burial
grounds, general stores, grey-planked barns painted with
See Ruby Falls, white-washed churches and one-room
schools, Burma Shave signs, creeks, gravel and mudhole
roads, and the old oak tree at Three Point.

Sacred site, the old home place is now a blank trudge
up a scrub-twined mountain, shrouded in choking
kudzu, a crumble of foundation in a tangle of blooming
honeysuckle, the old well filled in by decades of soil
sliding down the steep ridge and dried leaves from the
cool of the years, a porch rail buried under six inches of
hill soil.

Redeeming air, filled with the memory of logs drug out
of the forest by mules, split by saws at the town mill that
buzzed the life out of them, sawdust flying, settling, a
mound that grew taller than the one-story cottage next
door, taller than the church roof on the other side.

Holy water, flooded the schoolhouse where a girl trudged
morning and afternoon, mostly barefoot, her place to
shine, the brightest star in her constellation, the pot-
belly, a shadow on swollen floorboards, the slates broken,
forgotten.

Sacred site, the neighbor's two-story barn, weathered
with rain and age, still holds hay and memories of five
generations where a lifetime ago the girl and her brothers
stacked bales, she bossing them as always, stacking quick
as lightning.

Redeeming air, rich with the salvation of seeds nurtured
in a cold frame, fragile seedlings tucked in red earth, a fine
cash crop of burley come harvest, the sweat dried by then,
sunburns faded.

This legend-land claims a glory-filled homecoming every
year when laughter spirals into high mist, cold water seeps
from the spring of an uncomplicated mountain, walnuts
plummet from a stippled tree, and the old-time yawns
and stretches again.

Patsy Kisner

What I Can't Forget

Swaddled by
hills
and a vein
of creek
that keeps me
living,
my life
has evolved
into passion
for the roots
this farm
has given me,
until
the furrow turns
and raven black flint
exposes itself,
burns like
a woeful talisman
in my hand.

Elaine Fowler Palencia

The Kind of Town It Was

Standing in my crib alone upstairs in the dark
I'd wait to hear the cane tap-tap-tap
down the sidewalk across the street.
"Goodnight, Mr. Mauk!" I'd call.
"Goodnight," he'd quaver back. Then I could sleep.
I never saw him; Mother told me his name.

It was the kind of town where once, shifting veils
of green and gold lit the sky above the Kentucky hills,
the Northern Lights come to visit,
("Now that's something," people said),
like the pace car of the Indianapolis 500
briefly seen idling at one of our four stoplights
before sliding on out of town, a winged horse
or griffon briefly lighting down
("Now that's something else," people said).

In the town lived the small, balding music teacher
who had been a tail gunner in the war,
the manager of the lumberyard a bombardier,
the drama teacher a decoder in intelligence,
the photographer a survivor
of the Bataan Death March

And so the years went on,
like a bolt of fabric rolled out on the scarred counter
down at the dry goods store, to be measured, cut
and made into something serviceable,
a coat or dress worn by happenstance
when a small disguised god passed by.

Jeff Mann
Fehu 1/Abundance

It was everywhere
in those days, abundance,
like air, though, young
as I was, I could not see it,
could only take it for granted,
could only picture what was lacking,
what was missing, having not yet
known true want, the tedious
decays of age, the gasping suffocations.

Long before us in the familial
helix, said my father, there were
Mirkwoods, the Black Forest,
Baden-Württemberg,
the Germanic longhouse, longship,
the precious milk, the precious
cheese and meat and hides,
the worth of silver gauged
by counting heads of cattle.

Then our century: herds
of Hathor, our Herefords cropped
the fields, and the Forest Hill
soil my father cut open and sowed.
The seed, the seedling were his gods,
the coated-cotyledon miracle
of grain found in pyramids and coaxed
into sprouting after parched millennia.
Godsent? If not seed-spark, then what?

Appalachian country cornucopia,
the rhubarb and asparagus early,
then lettuce, spinach, peas, strawberries,
beets, cucumbers, kohlrabi, and later
tomatoes, beans, melons, potatoes, corn.
Like a mountain Frey, my father grew
all of it, and like mountain Friggas,
my grandmother, mother, aunt
put it up, jars and jars and jars
of spaghetti sauce, bread and butter
pickles, lime pickles, dilly beans,
Blue Lakes, corn relish, chowchow.
Those were our riches. Cash, my father
was wont to point out, no one can eat.

Fehu augurs mobile forms of wealth, say
the rune books. The Norns gave their gifts,
my family harvested green forms of fortune,
the horn of plenty foamed up and over.
Today, I draw Fehu on my forehead,
cut it into cheese, into home-baked bread,
pour mead into a shot glass set before
the long-cocked statue of Frey. Grizzled,
still I pray for fame, friends, sex, adventure,
money, stiff drink, and clan-shared fattening
feasts. Long before my checking account,
the little card-chip I slip into a machine
in Edinburgh, Reykjavik, London,
to purchase pub grub and pints,
there were Herefords back of the house,
bowls of wilted lettuce, fried green
tomatoes, and a cellar full of homegrown food.

Today, the last month of my fifties,
I browse Pulaski's farmers' market
and with green paper buy kohlrabi,
fried apple pies, and immaculate
bunches of collards. There, in their broad
green leaves, in the crooks of vein and rib,
Fehu abides, a rune-slew of abundance
cooking down with onion-broth and smoked
ham, stirred by a man still trying to learn
how to praise, who knows well how much
the gods deserve their due, how much
the gods rightfully detest a whining ingrate.

Kari Gunter-Seymour
By His Hands We Are Fed
Digital Photograph

Linda Parsons

Visitation: Frost

Though mid-October, the Best Boys are firm as softballs,
the kale will surely overwinter. A low of 38 last night, the
first real cold. I want to keep it going—even tomatoes
and greens want to go on until they burst their skins,
override the lattice border—so I cover the late garden
with a shower curtain and beach towel. From the
kitchen window, I blink and see instead the Atlantic, a
shrimp boat far out at sea. A large white dog in the same
sea paddles against the riptide, no headway to shore.
Swimsuited people shield their eyes. My granddaughter
terrified, like the rest of us, of the very bad end. This
was the scene on a Carolina beach some years ago, life's
anxious drama playing out before us. What was once
sure footing was suddenly unreachable. Ice-cold fear in
our hearts though we stood on burning sand in summer's
close heat. When day turns to bitter night in time's
blink, when something held dear ends seemingly out of
nowhere, we want to know the ground is under our feet
despite drought and grief and neglect. We want to ride
the waves to the lush horizon, even when there's no sheriff
to call and ski-doo us home to cheers and dry land. We
pull whatever we have from closet or shed to get through
because one morning soon we'll wake to a killing frost.
The plastic curtain has made a little shroud over the kale
and weeps condensation on the underside. I spread it on
the azaleas to dry in the shock of sun.

Wendy McVicker

Drownings

In these stories, whispered
or sung, someone always
drowns, usually

a woman, with flowing
braids. Brown

river, gray ocean, chasms
to cross without blinking.

Not everyone makes it
to shore, to freedom, to air

unburdened. Water
closes over bodies, but dying
voices are echoed

by gulls, by the low
moan of foghorns.

Some bodies are shattered
on the rocks, so close
to home.

(Is the land home?)

Some are turned back
unwanted: returned

to the salt sea, the mud-
laden river, sucking.

Those clouds above the water,
their last breath.

Valerie Nieman

Fusion

Water lipped high
in the bucket of blackberries,
floating off the bycatch
of hayseeds
and stink bugs.

A firefly struggled
across the surface,
wings wet,
forelegs combing
its tangled antennae.

I let it climb
onto my finger
and ferried it to a leaf,
(that nostalgia for sparks
rising to my cupped hands).

If I dumped berries,
insects, and all
into the kettle,
even one lightning bug's
electric fluid,

simmered with care,
might glow on the jam
like starlight across the great yawn
of galaxies, shining best
where it's blackest.

Eileen Rush

Celastrus orbiculatus
(Climbing Spindle Berry)

Melter of the limbs of trees, my love, you smelt
saplings where they spring up. All the sun is yours.
All the air. Every gap. If I were to unwind you now
from the spiral you have claimed, which loops around me
in woody circles from ankle to heart, the ways I healed
as I grew would be naked and smooth. The rest,
rough and shaggy bark. Where you rest, I am silk. I twist.
Unmanageable creature, I could never cut you off
close to your base, or smear your face with glyphosate.

Thomas Alan Orr

A Chainsaw Life

Seeing him in his overalls and red checkered earmuff cap,
a few teeth left in his big country grin,
you'd never guess he had a degree in forestry
until he talked about his craft—plainspoken
but erudite, not really caring if anyone listened.

Still gimpy after three surgeries in twelve months,
he fired up the chainsaw to harvest trees
on a private stand for meagre wages
and a day in the woods—quiet except for the saw—
a workhorse—thirty-two inch bar, seventy cee cee motor.

The sound bounced off trees for a mile,
a modulated buzz that rose and fell with the cut.
He could bring down a tree within a hair
of where he wanted it to land—a bit of artistry
in rough labor—rings exposed to read its age.

The saw was precious but firewood was gold –
hickory, oak, maple, ash—and his contempt
for softer woods palpable—hackberry, poplar, pine–
though he didn't insist that you agree—conviction
rooted in the quiet warmth of his Quaker faith.

Out where he lived, a snarling dog
chewed rabbit carcasses in the yard, the place
more hovel than house—gutters down,
upstairs window broken, foundation cracked. A spark
from the wood stove would level it quickly.

Those last years in the nursing home were hard.
From his window he could see the woods
and some days heard the sweet echo of a saw
wishing he were out there, wind in his face,
leaves whispering, at peace with trees.

*"Beech—pretty bark
—like paper—makes
fools think they
can write on it!"*

*"Cougars been gone a
generation, but I saw
tracks by the river.
People laugh!"*

*"Lotta folks don't know
squat about sharpening.
Keep that file angled in
the gullet of the tooth!"*

*"Not saying it won't burn.
"Sometimes you settle for
what you get—kind of like
life!"*

*"I was supposed to get the
the farm but was cut out of
the will. Family's the
cruelest animal in the
woods!*

*"Folks ask why take a good
tree down. There's a time
or growing and a time for
harvest—so for all of us."*

106

Sue Weaver Dunlap

This Morning at Dawn

Our front room holds quiet like an old woman wrapped shawl tight, deep-seated in her rocker, Poppy's Bible open in her lap. Faded eyes search out reminders of home sheltered behind a glass-doored curio. Tokens of past lives scent her heart. She conjures Charlie Goode's fingers pressing Prince Albert cherry tobacco into his walnut pipe, his long hands shaky deep into his gloaming hour of leaving. Her well-worn small snuff tin holds its place high on its own shelf, her pocket tin long absent from her apron pocket, a thimble long past quilting and mending chores. She waits in gathering dark for Mama to call her home with lonesome tunes on a harmonica dark and old.

Vanda Galen
Eye on Main

Digital Photograph

Richard Tillinghast

To Find the Farm

It couldn't have disappeared off the map
because it was never on
the map.

A half-forgotten map led me there
past the Baptist church and the country store,
through woods and across the L&N tracks.

But the farm had been erased.
Chicken house, corncrib, milking stalls,
barn cats, John Deere tractor,

a rat terrier named Pal.
A shed full of tools, a plough,
mules that brayed and balked.

I couldn't take it in. I stood and looked
for the assemblage of labor, the continuum
of seed and soil, weather and muscle,

the intelligence it takes to grow things—
all this that lived here
through bondage, invading armies, hard times.

A farmer and his wife,
half-a-dozen tenants in unpainted shacks.
Cotton picked, ginned, and sold.

Tina Parker

The Before Time

Each time I came to
There were more people
In the room
They fell to their knees
Spoke in tongues
Lined out hymns
Granny brought 'sang
For my female weakness
She said but still I could not
Get out of bed

Used to be
I'd go with her
I had a quick eye
For all matter of roots
And kept my wits about me
In the woods
Now I ask for catmint
To calm my nerves
For cohosh to ease
The cramps
The nurses mumble
And bring more bromide
They curse and spit
The word Witch
Then leave the room
Before I can ask again.

Rachel Anne Parsons

Starletta

When her grandmother was a little girl,
the passenger pigeons were so common,
her great-grandfather would shoot dozens
as they flocked over their fields.
Only smaller birds survive in such number
these days, bejeweled little shadows
that land in the garden and ravage the seeds
fresh-planted by Starletta's own hand.

The birds have the gift of noise,
a cloud of sound that descends and reminds
Starletta of children in hallways,
cackling laughter that echoes in her head.
Some people might shoot a gun
to silence that sound, but to her,
cacophony is sacred.
Life is noise and silence is death.
Better to hear the screaming birds
than to sit alone in the day room
without a sound.

James Shipman
Interview with a Woman
About to Be Sawed in Half

Mixed media sculpture
Original Photo Credit: Seton Hill College Artist Book, *Image Song*
(1994)

Walt Peterson

Interview with a Woman
About to Be Sawed in Half

My daddy spoke nothin' but Mill Hunky.
Then Sister Celeste tried to teach me Latin,
told me men tapped a heat in the open hearth
flames above the mill were Tongues of Fire.
First time the carney came to town,
I knew what I had to do. The second
I packed my teddy bear, a pair of jeans,
my rosary beads and said goodbye to
a town named after a Goddamn mill.

Mines and mills and unions,
that's all my family could talk, so I hooked up with the show.
Nothin' personal, you know,
just I had it up to here, and
the circus and carney and stage
have been with me ever since.
Tell me, what's so bad about that: followin' the sun
on the tilt of the earth like balls
in a pinball machine headin' for bright lights?
The fat bearded lady and tattooed man
showed me who to trust and who just
wanted time and money and my body.
They's the best parents a girl could want.
They taught me how to separate rubes from their money
with a smile. Like Gypsies we hit a town
and I'm real cute and sweet-faced too.
And we'd go door to door takin' pictures
of kids and family portraits

(I got real good, even if I do say so.)
Them pictures was real cheap,
but the frames, they's awful expensive,
and I'd be a little jealous, too, because
there's nobody to want to take and buy a picture for me.
I felt sorriest for women
who had to have a picture of their baby.
They were like the women
in my Ohio river town, lovin' their family
tryin' to do what's right. But I got a right to eat too.

One winter in Sarasota, I joined the circus,
left the bearded lady and the tattooed man.
I loved the carney and Mary and Stanley.
Don't get me wrong! When you know
it ain't for you, you leave or get old fast.

I still got my legs & smile & wits, too
and elephant shit and sawdust in my veins
and on my shoes, and now
I work for Magic Zoltan.
Some nights I outlive knives,
some I float through flaming hoops
and for a finale get stuffed in boxes and
get cut in two.
You know I trust Zoltan,
his hands like a surgeon's.
And I know what you're thinkin'
'cause I got a dirty mind
just like you—but neither he nor I
wants to eat where we shit.

We're just friends, the man
with beautiful hands and the lady
with legs too nice to separate from this smile,
to be cut in two.
Believe me, that blade comes close.
I'm too smart to let it come
between my Art and a jealous lover.

And, yeah, I've known a man or two,
Jo-Jo the Dog-face Boy and Max
The Wild Animal King to name a few.

For my money, Jo-Jo had it all;
he was a sweet, sweet man
who knew how it felt to be hurt and ugly,
so I gave him a whirl,
but he taught me, my God, he taught me
tenderness and love that goes beyond just need. Max?
He wasn't all he was cracked up to be.

Max shot blanks if you know what I mean.
Even his big cats didn't love him
like you'd think.

Well, I'm getting long-winded
like I know the meaning of it all.
And once on a train between Joplin and Sioux Falls,
I thought I had that meaning.
I was sittin' on the can
lookin' at the cover on a catalogue
that showed a family and some others.

And they was starin' and pointin' right out of that cover:
laughin' and pointin' at me
like they'd do at a circus or zoo
for monkeys or hippos or us.
But now I was lookin' back, and I could see right under SEARS
how damn funny they was, too.

Yeah, life is a slight-of-hand, smoke and mirrors,
dog and pony circus with sharp blades whirrin' through the air.
You just got to decide who's real and who's show
at the end when it's time to go.

Dale Marie Prenatt

Ghost Light

In its bare glow   stoic as Greek marble
               I dedicated my life to
the great Temporal   Art
The Theatre demands it
Tasseled cords   wound me
under the beam of a Cyclops   I unspooled
myself as he slept   I slept
           Temporal Arts:
      music's timely phases   poetry's faces
I was born
under the Balsamic Moon   Slivery blade
Born at the river's crescent   at two oh two
                Black linen
             sky pinned
        over ancient folds
Born for working   in the dark

Sarah Pross

Night Road

I drive country roads, wait
for the magic moment
when the sun goes down,
houselights come on.
We are all the same, now,
in my mind,
want to be home with kin,
gathered around supper tables.
It doesn't matter,
the extravagant poorness
of the front yards here.
The dark hides—
cars on blocks, overgrown yards.
Soft light spills from living room
windows onto broken glass sidewalks.

Marianne Mersereau

Sonnet for the Pit Ponies

Gus, Rufus, Charlie and Pip, turned out to starve
on the blasted tops of the blue ridges
after spending most of your lives underground,
you were hand fed, never learned to crop grass.

You pulled cars loaded with coal to the surface
till Nineteen Thirty-Five when you were replaced
by machines that did the work for you
and you left behind miners who loved you—

miners like my uncle who fed you from
his lunch pail—half a sandwich, a piece of cake
or apple core, and offered to give you a home
but the company turned him down and

you spent your retirement years like he did,
struggling to breathe with dust-covered lungs.

Bonnie Proudfoot

Doorway to Nowhere

Because they were perfect in their own ways,
        these mutts we found or maybe they found us
because they had eyes of clarified butter
because their noses were called to dirt
because of their fur, coats whose moats
        we inhaled, swapped essences with,
because cremation changes the state of being
        to ether and dust
because daffodils will grow
because daffodils are blooming now
because they found each other in life
        like sisters of soul
because the clay was so dense
        and the days were so hot and the only sound left
        was the mattock as it chopped through roots of hemlock
because it felt like duty
        to climb downhill through the woods to the creek
        and heft slate stones
because a doorway opens to nowhere
because there is a land of myth and dream
because there is no school for letting go.

Jim Minick

When the Ground Disappears

Fog settles in, and suddenly my morning is more.
The woods drip, making the hollow even quieter. On
the ridge, a solitary nuthatch. Closer, a gray squirrel eats
an acorn, teeth scritching. All sound muffled, all sight
muted. No more Iron Mountain, miles away, just Wooded
Hill, a quarter-mile close, its tallest poplar a silhouette
against the white.

What magic do you hold, dear Fog? Are you
water? Are you air? I breathe you, yet I don't drown.
I drink you and yet thirst. A pileated cackles close by.
The woodpecker could be ten feet away, the soup so
thick, dense enough to hide the bird's black and white
bigness, its flame-topped head. All the while, blue jays
condescend. Fall is theirs as they graze the treetops, acorns
filling craw and gullet. Acorns fueling blue. Jay calls
jabbing the air as they fly oak to oak. They look like they
have goiter, the craws so full. And fog just drifts along.
Making mountains disappear. Muting the sun, but not
the jay.

Another morning, clouds heavy and low, with a
sliver of silver between the sky's gray and the mountains'
blue. The clouds move solid like a tectonic plate, only
faster. If they get any lower, they'll clip the mountains,
boom, a thousand feet cut off, maybe more, all in a day.

Then it'll be us. A gray rolling plate to grind us
down into the dust we already are. At the speed they're
moving, it wouldn't take long.

But I guess if the sky lowered anymore, it would

be fog. And Fog, you don't grind, do you? You just consume without consuming.

And there, for a moment, the sun cracks through that sliver.

It has this habit of focusing us, fog does. Gone are the colored hillsides. Gone the rivers and ravines. Everything gone but fog and us. In that vastness, fog frees us to grapple with what's inside. To fog, though, inside and outside are the same, so it asks, Why such sadness? And when we don't respond, it says, I'll leave soon as the sun comes up, but for now, listen. The heart is its own sun. The heart can burn me away. The heart is its own little ember of hope.

Fog again, though more distant. Even the pines on Wooded Hill are gray. The ravens fly by, blackness white-tinged and muted. Everything south of Wooded Hill, the next ridges and far Iron Mountain, are gone. Gone like the old year, gone like so many dead, gone like yesterday.

But if I walked south, I'd eventually find those mountains, eventually have to climb them. So they're not really gone, are they? Can we say that about the dead?

Yes, I believe we can.

Fog blinds us; fog makes us see.

That larger world behind all that is here—fog makes that spirit world physical: I feel it—moist on my cheeks, cool in my nose, dewdrops on my lashes. When a slip of fog drifts up the valley, I see wind. When I walk the foggy ridge, the very ground disappears, and I become aware, finally, that I am surrounded by spirit. I breathe pneuma with every breath.

To live a wakeful life—to live in each now—is to embrace a certain blindness, because fog offers no other way, no other time, no time at all.

Find me, Fog, and lose me. And loose me.

Erin Miller Reid

Mother Tongue

Nary'ne on that,
Marty Gilley said when the teacher asked
how many multiplication facts he'd done.

Nary'ne,
a foreign word to sixth grade ears,
a leaf-rustling, brush-crashing word
that sent titters rippling desk to desk.

It means no,
our teacher translated, defended Marty
even though Marty hadn't done his math homework.

Nary'ne on that,
such a heavy way to say
No
None
Not
like rolling a cinderblock into a pond to
drown the meaning.

But what it meant was
a pepper-haired Memaw took Marty
under her housecoated wing, fried him a skillet of ham
and cabbage,
tucked him in under a quilt she patched herself, and said
Nary'ne on that,
when he asked if he could stay up for Johnny Carson
on late night TV.

None of us talked like television either.
We asked the kid next to us to *reach me* a pencil,
if the teacher *cared to* help us figure a square root.
We picked a *buggy* at the grocery store,
said *I might could* come over tomorrow.
g's dropped and currented away into the eddies of the larynx,
i's leaned back, lolling against tonsils,
a's stretched up to caress the soft palate,
the vowels like a sprawled out, porch-sittin' Papaw resting
    his eyes.

Thirty years gone and
now even the county kids talk like they're giving the
    six-o-clock news.
Their tongues clackity clack,
lips tight, precise,
drawstringed at the corners.
No *i*'s sounding like *ah*'s,
a's and *o*'s streamlined bullets from their mouths.

The other day my five-year-old asked
"Mama, can I have a *drank* of water?"
Not drink, *drank.*
A drank of water. A drank.
I drank that up, drank it in.
Drank.
Drank.
Thank.
Thankful for the imprints
of ancestors on our tongues.

Pam Campbell

Finding Mama

One: Raven

Wildflowers waved their yellow and white heads, stirred by my sturdy, four-year-old feet. I chased butterflies until tired. Nestled between boulder and earth, I slumbered with deer and fawn.

I woke to white cloud-sails puffing across blue sky and remembered Mama. She let go of me, caressing the white dog instead. Her coal-black hair tumbled around her bowed face and closed eyes in a peek-a-boo gone wrong.

My fingers curled around the rock heart Mama gave me. An ache swelled but I blinked it away. Holding my rock heart close to my beating one, I counted my steps back to Mama. One, two, three. One, two, three.

I cooled my feet in a little creek where swooping branches of willow kissed the ground and wept with me. Sooty birds stretched across sunset sky, steady wingbeats, accordion folding and unfolding until they too were gone. Moonlight softened darkness, cradled and caressed. Whippoorwill chanted a lullaby.

The ravens broke day with me, melodic, deep *Kraa, Kraa.* One flew upside down, another somersaulted. I extended my arms and flew with them to Mama.

Dandelions dangled from my fingertips, a fairy's crown for Mama. I counted my steps back to Mama. One, two, three. One, two, three.

Two: Bluebird

I came to live with Mammaw and Daddy Pa when I was four because Mama lost me lots.

Daddy and I rode to them in Ruby, the car I named, my front-seat home. I snuggled close to Daddy, full of cereal eaten straight out of the box, and silly songs: *Oh, Pam Campbell is a bag of wind. She's got big feet and a double chin.* He sang sweet songs, too. One had me singing to every robin I chanced across afterwards: *When the red, red, robin comes bob, bob, bobbin' along, sweet song.* He taught the sounds and shapes of spirituals: *Swing low, sweet chariot, comin' for to carry me home.* He sang lead and I followed.

I didn't see Daddy much. His job, setting up stores for Winn Dixie, kept him on the road. During Thanksgiving and Christmas visits, my tongue got confused and I called him Daddy-Pa instead of Daddy. He didn't mind. Neither did Daddy-Pa when after Daddy left, my tongue got mixed up again.

Daddy came the night before I was to start first grade with a bag of school supplies, a brand-new box of crayons, wide-lined paper, and yellow pencils with brown rubber tops that erased mistakes.

You got your worry wrinkles on, baby girl.

I'd rather stay home with Mammaw. Daddy Pa reads to me every night. I make words for him.

Daddy Pa's done a good job but there's other things you'll learn from Miss Wilson. She taught me. She's a peach.

Daddy called the people he liked the most "a peach." I liked apples best but agreed to give school a try.

Miss Wilson hugged Daddy like Mammaw did when Daddy strode in her front door after a long time away. And Miss Wilson hugged me, like I was hers. I never noticed Daddy leaving once Miss Wilson put a book in my hand. Daddy Pa taught me the sounds and shapes of words. When Miss Wilson heard the letters sing on my tongue she moved me to the bluebird reading group, my favorite bird. She was like another Mammaw to me.

I wished for Mama to come that day, too, but she didn't. On Mammaw's drop-leaf table, there's a picture of Mama and Daddy, taken before I was born. In it, Mama is sitting in the curve of the crescent moon with Daddy.

Daddy, how'd you and Mama get to the moon?
I lassoed it and drew it to earth for us…
His laugh faded. I kept his words in my heart and didn't ask anymore.

Mama came once when I was seven.
Hey, Pam.
I sidled up to Mammaw.
I'm your Mama, don't you remember me?
I didn't. She looked different than when she sat on the moon with Daddy. Mammaw made us all a cup of tea and eased us into knowing each other again. By nightfall, I was on Mama's lap at the piano, she making the notes with my fingers on top of hers, us making music together.

I begged to skip school the next morning but Mama coaxed me with a promise to play the piano with me right after school. She tied the brand new shoes she bought for me and shooed me out just as my cousin hollered *hurry up*.

She was gone when I got home. I didn't cry, just curled up like a roly-poly, all quiet-like, in my bed. Mammaw let me be and covered me, shoes and all, with a soft blanket.

Mama disappeared into the letters she wrote in her left-handed slant, into the pictures she drew and colored, into the worn record she sent of Captain Kangaroo singing *Button Up Your Overcoat You Belong To Me*, and into the moon with Daddy. I traced the shape of them and tried to remember when we were all together.

No one shaped the word *divorce*. Not telling the truth of what is real hurts, even if meant in kindness.

Three: Grackle

The summer I was nine, my daddy visited with a woman that wasn't my mama. She drew me on her lap, colored pictures, and sang songs. That night, when Daddy tucked me in bed, he asked if I liked her. I said yes. A few months later, I learned the shape of the word *regret*.

Daddy married her and I went to live with them and three step-sisters—a three-year-old, a five-year-old, and a nine-year-old with a first name like mine. Those children were the ones Daddy knew about. I learned with Daddy that this woman had another daughter and a son who lived in Texas with their daddy.

My skin learned the shape of the words *bruised, bloodied, welted,* my ears the shape of *curses* from the woman that I was to call "Mama" but who was monster, not mama to me. My Daddy with new babies to hold and a job from daybreak to dark, saw me no more. The worse trickery of all.

I learned the shape of the word *lush* from my stepsister, six months younger than me. She taunted—*I know things about your mother that you don't know.* Even though I didn't know the meaning of the word *lush*, her saying it boiled a rage, and in a split-second I was on top of this stepsister who knew the language of fist-fighting better than me. I didn't hit her. Just pinned her arms and shook her, telling her to take the word back, knowing by her smirk it wasn't a good word.

I disappeared into carrying babies on hips too small, washing and waxing floors with hands too small, and tried not to stoke a fire in "Mama," which happened anyway. I disappeared into books and woods. I hid books so she wouldn't take them and hid tears when she decided summer visits to Mammaw and Daddy Pa spoiled me.

She destroyed the letters from my real mama and refused her phone calls. I learned the shape of the word *cruel*.

Four: Cardinal

I was 58 years old and grief-stricken by Daddy's death. In my hand was the picture of Mama and him on the crescent moon found deep in Daddy's safe with a letter from Mama: *I know you brought your new girl to meet Pam. I know I can't take care of her but be careful. She has been through so much.*

I hungered to know more and wished she was alive to ask. I dug deeper in Daddy's safe and found more pieces of Mama: photos with Daddy, my grandparents, and the justice of the peace who joined a Jolly with a Campbell, cards with sweet words, a baby book, and two slender pages that dissolved what had begun on the crescent moon that Daddy lassoed for them.

The baby book was a happy find. I didn't know it existed. Mama chronicled visits to and from grandparents, my colds, my teething, my first through fourth birthdays, and her thoughts: *Pam is a happy baby. She claps her little hands when the birds sing.* It was like peering through a window into a room full of light and belonging. I breathed in parts of my life that had been erased.

I didn't know where she was buried but I was determined to find Mama. I searched by Internet hopeful that her small hometown newspaper would hold a paragraph about her death because of a title she won, significant in a small mill town. The newspaper granted her two paragraphs. I learned a year before her marriage to my father and two years before my birth, she was chosen Miss Gaffney. Her talent: pianist. She went forward in competition and was chosen first runner-up in the Miss South Carolina pageant.

I learned she played classical and gospel music, loved flowers and cooking. I learned where she was buried. I drove across three states to find her, in a quiet cemetery, nestled in the foothills of the Blue Ridge Mountains of South Carolina.

There was no one to ask where a woman, once bright and full of dreams of music, marriage, and babies, was buried. Overwhelmed and unsure of where to start, I marked it off into grids, sectioned by loops of paved road.

As the sun crawled from eastern to noonday sky, my body relaxed into the cadence of a thorough and detailed pace. A cardinal's *cheer, cheer, cheer, birdie, birdie, birdie* broke the stillness.

This was a modest graveyard marked with flat, granite gravestones. No mausoleums or monuments, no obelisks or chest-guarding angels here. I noted names, birthdates and death years and counted my steps through marked passage of times, row after row, after row.

Sound and visual bites of memory mingled with cardinal's song until he was muted, grayed in the background of memory. Four-year-old feet once roamed these hills with a dark-headed mother until lost from one another. Papaw and Grandma Jolly lived not far from here, in a white-framed house sandwiched between a private airstrip and their barbeque restaurant. Grandma Jolly raised chickens, made fine barbeque and chewed snuff. Papaw was tall with a full head of white hair and a laugh that lifted smiles.

By noon, my clothes were sweat-soaked, my throat parched. I regretted not carrying my water but didn't want to lose my place in the grid-search to fetch it from my car. I kept at it, determined to find Mama. *Just like when I was little, Mama. I was always trying to find you.*

A flicker, like a movie reel come undone, flapped pieces of dark images: Mama and her friends playing cards and drinking out of clear jars, their words getting louder and louder, a man staggering towards me—*You're a pretty little thing, ain't you?* and me running and hiding, losing Mama. I shoved these memories back. *I just want to find Mama.*

The sun was lowering into western sky when I found her. She was nestled amongst her kin. Kin who breathed in whisps of faces remembered deep in the bone of me. Papaw and Grandma Jolly, Aunt Doris and her husband, Uncle D.C., Aunt Vivian, and Uncle Dubb—the name I called him, not the name on his gravestone. The joy and triumph of finding her burst from me in four-year-old voice: *I found you, Mama.*

In sunset's last rays, I picked dandelions, yellow heads dotting the green grass. I weaved a fairy crown for

Mama. I traced her name lingering on the middle name I share with her and placed her crown on it. Three single dandelions were in my damp, warm fist. I brought them close to my heart. An ache swelled but I didn't blink it away.

What happened to us, Mama?

I touched Mama's name one last time and laid the three dandelions in the center of her dandelion crown, one for her, one for Daddy, and one for me.

Mike Wilson

Papaw and Mamaw Say I Do

She was sixteen, picking beans
when he rode in on a black stallion
literally swept her off her feet
    claiming
her against her family's wishes but
in accordance with her own

                    they galloped

to Tennessee.

He was a dirt farmer who made everything
with his hands: a house, furniture in it,
a barn to house tobacco

                    She grew a garden
apples, cherries, grapes to feed six kids
in a holler too poor to afford a high school
cleaned and washed and cooked and canned
every moment filled with work except for
church

        He was close-mouthed, couldn't risk
wasting words, but made her fix a full dinner
for every visitor who dropped in, even when
they lacked food enough to feed themselves

                   She sewed
so much it would have made a mortal blind
but store-bought was for people with money

134

except

after selling the crop, if he let her, she'd buy
a pretty to treasure.

He was Republican in a county of Democrats, too
young for World War I, too old for World War II,
tenor in a gospel quartet, drank whiskey when he
could get it, harbored judgments he kept to himself.
His voice could strike like a hickory stick on her
and the children, but never the grandchildren.

Theirs was marriage when husbands and wives
didn't talk like characters in a novel or
need to dress up love in words
                                        still

she imagined what he could have said
she wished she could have heard.

Amy Wright

Breech

winds sculpt shorelines
in ice-sheened   snowmelt,

drift
                    bad time to labor
                     & not her first twisted
        calf
                    Doc Taylor unavailable this round, hurt his hip
                            hard way to make a living
                            J said last time he chased the dam
                                across the field
                    shot a tranquilizer gun,
                                        missed,
                            aimed again
        pained her to run
                    though she could not trust a man,

                    he pulled her calf, she healed

        a single hoof
                    now in her backside   wrong side up

                    nearby earth laced red, to push she stands

                        the horse vet in West Virginia,

                        or she would come

                                slick chain in the barn

        but no darts

          or stomach
      to cut out
  a dead calf
    surely dead,
          drowned in the broken
               afterbirth

nothing to do, we tell ourselves

             she might expel it,
              let the hand
      imperfect
        formed her womb
    turn it for her
 though the churn
 would be miraculous, we sleep

      moon still out
        at dawn   when we go to her
      by the stream   she sits, a stoic pharaoh

that long night alone
    who birthed this gold   field
      all the blinding light
        on the snow
   hers

   gray as cemetery stone
   in a thatch of limbs, her stillborn

    not a mother's triumph,

    to be the one to live.

Poem first published in *Grist,* Issue 14

Dana Wildsmith

Sight

You're fey, of course. Bound to be—
Irish on both sides,
Patten and Tierney. Daddy could *see*.
It's why he drank. Besides,

as soon as you decided to talk
when you were nearly two,
you said things you really ought not
know at only two.

They told me before I came here,
you'd answer when I asked,
as if I'd know who They were.
I watched you after that

because of Daddy, but you were fine,
until you weren't. You'd dream
about a friend and call to find,
sure enough, something

was going wrong for her. You thought
her rough spot was yours,
since you could see it, but it's not.
Honey, maybe by now you've learned

you just can't carry all the hurt
in the world. Now I don't mean
pretend it isn't there, but your
job should be to clean

it up and make it usable,
then move on. The trash
that's dumped along our road? We haul
off what's no good and stash

the treasures—two-by-fours, a sink,
kittens— until we find
a home for them. Sweetheart, I think
every time you write

a poem you're finding a home for grief,
stitching it like squares
for a quilt. Your grandmother couldn't *see,*
but she could quilt, so there's

your double inheritance: hands
rooted in life to bind
your mind in a way your granddaddy's
wasn't. You're lucky, child.

Susan Shaw Sailer

Still Laced with Hope

She's not a captive yet. Baby on her back,
her legs bridge promise and despair. Sole
on her sandal gone, she unties the shoe,
kicks it to one side of the dusty path, altar
to her church of freedom. She knows
the route. Her brother in Georgia coached her,
quizzed her, until she got it right, each bend,
each fork. Fourteen miles today. Her foot
without the sandal bleeds. She works
dust into the wound, stops for the night,
gives her breast to Juana. Day after tomorrow
she'll reach the Rio Grande, walk across it,
river running low. And then? Yesterday
she heard across the border people with guns
take children from their parents, don't give
them back. She'd die without Juana,
Juana without her. She knew about robbers
when she started, didn't know she might
lose Juana. Fears leap at her, invade her sleep.
She sees the night she left her village, Juan
dead in the road before their home, the hole
between his eyes still bleeding—he wouldn't
join the gang. Toward east, dawn. Whose
daughter can she be now, parents dead,
brother last week rounded up, deported.
She fingers her rosary, says morning prayers.
Juana's hungry. She gives suck, gets up.
Miles back to Guatemala, 1,550. Goes on.

Roberta Schultz

Drive-by Sonetto

On the Day of the Dead I head back home,
drive south on York Street to the train track wall,
turn right at the ghosts of pool and school yard
where our shotgun house stands guard. There's
the street sign we poled May Days, climbed July
nights, dared December licks. No trees out front
nor shack in the back now cradle fledgling broods.
New landlords tumble old nests, make grottos
where Mother Mary rears stone eyelids,
hears rote prayers. Still, our voices clatter
around the table, escape like ragged birds,
flutter over the transom toward twilight.

Grandma Babe cackles above passenger train din,
No one in this house ever had a pot to piss in.

Gerald Smith

Oaks

City child had no idea,
Measure of experience or store of memory
To walk sent but unguided by me
To scan and count a cemetery laid to east
Two hundred years ago
Beneath wide *Quercus stellata*, post oak
Called Christian oak for its cruciform leaves
Planted or saved by first settlers
Who made home and farm, life and death
Beside a great spring
And set aside this place, small hill, and tree
Where the graves kept pace with the lives
And then outran the living
Where gravestones spilled the hilltop
And filled all the spaces under the trees.

So she worked and marked,
Counted names and dates:
Loving mother, War of 1812, Asleep in Jesus
I am the resurrection and the life.
Good student, good data; field report later tonight
Until at once she stopped and ran to me crying
"Have you seen all these short graves?"
As her heart broke with insight.
No lecture needed from me,
No chapter to read of
"Infant mortality in the upland South"
She knew before learning, beyond instruction
The sorrows on this hill
Deeper than the shade of oaks.

Joyce Compton Brown

After the Diagnosis

The man and woman are walking the dog
together in the drizzling rain,
the dog pushing, pulling,
sniffing for new pleasures, as dogs do,
its little brown butt, short smooth tail
wobbling in the mist.

They are giving it some leash,
knowing that life is finite,
that all in all, joys come down
to touching a hound's floppy velvet ears,
seeing the same ordinary world together,
one sniff, one smile, one wag.

And that is what remains—
not the prayers, the casseroles,
the kindly cards, the ritual to come—
only the grasp of a moment
in the commonest of household chores,
to hold onto like a sepia photo.

His pants hang loose on stalk legs.
The two walk in tiny short steps,
each one slow-savored.
He arches thin and tall, holding the umbrella
over her bare head, getting damp himself,
protecting her from the drizzle.

The little mutt tugs, the umbrella's
flowers—poppies, daffodils, bluets,
and daisies—circle above them.
He hovers his umbrella
above her, its speckled motley
blossoms soft-silken above their heads.

Annette Sisson

To See Small Fish Hanging
in High Branches

My eyeballs' curvature feathers the forest.
I choose precision binoculars, barium
glass crisping texture and edge.
This crystal amplifies the air's flux
of lumens, gathers them up
like stray contours and plumes.
A bird forms in bouquets of light.

Without prisms, I see hawks
circle a blue afternoon, their tails
ablaze; a yellow-mauve iris,
the veins of its beard geometric
etching on sepal; the fluttering hem
of a cloudy lake; the startling girth
of a heron's nest lofted in sycamore.

The heron nestlings call for glass.
Its mesmeric gaze. To pierce the sky,
to see the heads bob, the parents'
talons, their powder down, the blue-
grey vigil as they tend the glossy
chicks—nebs, and tongues, and glints
of small fish in high branches.

Randa Shannon

Old Love

I wake to your voice. On my lips.
Rustling window curtain, sly conjure,
The moon's at the clouds again. I heed
my ghosts, even those not dead, just gone.

I wrap for the chill of autumn night
go out to the hilltop field, the wide
gash of open sky, once our summer school.
You taught the constancy of heaven.
When the moon would rise. When, Venus.
When stars would fall. Mercury at dawn.

We teased a slutty waxing hunchback moon,
gave all her clinging clouds stripper names,
hid in night shade by the honeysuckle fence.
I built fire, laid out a blanket made
for prayer and told my mother's snake tales.
I taught the ephemera of golden moss.

The moon is full tonight. Simple.
Clouds breaking thin. Vines bare.
Earth hard. And I am here alone.
What love I have now wants no paramour.
It is flung wide and random, unmade
and feral as the red foxes, yipping
in the brambles below the ridge.

An old woman on a bright night hilltop
I give the fox my urgent rasp and bark
yes the dark hunt   *yes yes* the changeling earth
yes moons of Jupiter, green winter mosses yes yes

Sherry Cook Stanforth

While my newly-widowed mom
watches icicles melt

from the kitchen window, she prays for March
to bring its lion's roar—*just no more white*
death pouring down on our heads, then scoots
her chair into a warm patch of light, saying *we've*
all had plenty of winter's hard slice, with tree limbs
snapped clean off, littering up the backyard…even
birds seem erased from the sky. For weeks, we've
studied water's many transformations—rain
turning to sleet, or snow deep enough
to bury all traces of backyard garden
beds—and today, the house eaves
sprout rows of hooked fingers,
gilded but split tongues, gnarled
stalactites glittering in deadly
afternoon prisms. Each drip-
drip-drip runs an up-tempo
course we know cannot last.
Any minute they are going
to fall, Mom says, though
this keen vigil feels
so very slow—
this waiting
for time
to break
into its

clear-
cut
end.

Colette Tennant

Tracks

I tell my students illustrators almost always
focus on the jaws, the fangs,
the exaggerated drool.

In some versions, the wolf
eats the grandmother but not Little Red.
In others, they're both gobbled up.

My class likes the happier one,
where the woodsman comes along,
carefully cuts open the full belly,

pulls out Red and Grandmother too,
although students don't mention
their naked resurrection.

Then there's the one where Little Red
outwits the wolf, runs as fast as anything
hunted can run, just beats him to her own front door.

That day she learned the hard lesson
about that twilight hour,
when a thing becomes its own shadow,

and its hunger becomes its own story,
and my students lean into what she sees
because they see it too.

Sam Campbell

Jacob Plays Guitar

Digital Photograph

Dick Westheimer

A Jam Man's Last Breath

I'm told Vernon is on a vent—
the wind-up-woosh and monitor beeps
sing to him like he used to sing
"Blue Eyes Crying"—in the key of E
just like Willie. He crooned it smooth
like an Opry star. Every week
we'd circle up, Bill would hammer-on
his nicked-up Martin's A string like

a heartbeat breathes into my chest,
draws out Vernon's voice which,
like an ember, warmed the room. But
that one song was not enough
to keep him coming back so we'd see
him less and less until I missed
the song so much I learned it,
badly I was told. Somehow my beat
was too square to capture the sorrow
a rightful singer of this song knows, which was
made clear when Vernon returned, sang it like

I loved it. Who knew he'd be the first
among us to wind up alone, in a room
with a machine-made rhythm that
played in the key of whatever
the device hummed. When he rasped
a last grinding exhale just before
they slipped the tube down his throat,
no one asked the name of the last song
he'd sung.

Ace Boggess

One Foot Dancing

When I look back at those actions
I've read will take ten years off my life—

I should've died yesterday,
should've died half a century before I was born.

Measure each outlandish wheeze
my squeezed throat offers.

I'm still at it, failing to study warning labels,
eat right, exercise. Somewhere

there's a field of tobacco planted in my honor,
a pill factory now shut down.

I'm tired, crackling in ankles, knees, & back.
So much left to accomplish,

& music reminds me to maintain
one foot dancing though it hurts.

Chuck Stringer

Time Machine

Today, picking up a knapped chert flake, I see
that South Fork's hand of flowing mystery
has set back the dial on the creek wash
one thousand years. And though I've walked
this way many times, it takes the cleansing
action of a late night one-inch rain to make
a muddy flake flash its name in August daylight.
I listen to a field sparrow singing in the distance,
like the man who once crouched here listened
over each loud crack when again and again
he struck a sediment's hard fist with his hammer-
stone. A few steps later, I spy the telltale
contoured shape of a fossil brachiopod, perfectly
preserved and waiting—just as it waited on
the bottom of an Ordovician sea—waiting
for me four hundred million years to come here,
pick it up, hold it with the chert in my hand,
and revel in the time that together we travel.

Llewellyn McKernan

Creek Time

I walk by Four Pole
late in the afternoon when
the sun points its long finger

at drowsy tree-banks and
clouds heavy as deeds drop
anchor on the bottom. My

shadow, moving as if asleep,
falls face down in front of me,
eating the dust with each step

I take forward, going in circles
around Four Pole as it swims
a crooked seam. How near

they are—the hills that crowd
this valley, reality that crowds
my dreams as they topple and

fall into water wave-strung
and bewildered, casting no
shadow as my own shadow

guides me—a soft gray body,
light as a cloud, yet it pulls me
along like some silent note in

an unknown song, lightening
the grasp of gravity so nothing
is left but the ripple of water

and even that gets thinner,
dimmer, the shade deeper,
sweeter for everything grows

dark except for the moon's
sliver of light floating me
on a silver surface.

Scott Goebel

Remembering
Founding Publisher Robb Webb

I first crossed paths with Robb Webb near the
old sand quarry at his brother Jim's Pine Mountain
home nearly 20 years ago. He was kind, gracious and I
quickly thought he had a great radio voice, warm and
familiar, just like Jim. Driving home an hour later it hit
me that I had heard that rich voice hundreds of times.
When Nelson Robinette Webb died in New York City
this winter, we lost yet another remarkable voice and
an essential part of the long history of this journal, *Pine
Mountain Sand & Gravel* (*PMS&G*). While readers and
scholars are likely aware that Jim Webb was the founding
editor of this journal, fewer know that his brother,
Robb, in addition to being the long-time voice of *60
Minutes* and *The CBS Evening News* with Scott Pelley,
was this journal's founding publisher. Without Robb's
guidance and support, the early issues of this journal may
have never come to life. And it goes deeper than that;
Robb was likely the last surviving employee of the Pine
Mountain Sand & Gravel company—driving a dump
truck for his Uncle Gordy in summers as a teenager.

Webb was born on January 29, 1939 at the
family's home in Whitesburg, Kentucky, and grew up
mostly in Shadyside, Ohio. The Webb family returned to
Letcher County while Robb was in college at Ohio State.
In 1959, he hitched a ride to California and after a time
enlisted in the Army. His media career began in Asmara,
Eritrea with Armed Forces Radio and Television where he
directed and produced television news, a Dick Clark-type

dance party program, and was also a disc jockey on the radio station. After two years, he returned to Fort Sam Houston as an information specialist, interviewing troops in the Western United States—those one-minute snippets some of us remember during the evening news.

After the Army, Webb took a daytime DJ job with KITE in San Antonio, started a family and joined the Alley Theatre in Houston as a company member and resident photographer. After two seasons he moved to New York to study and advance his acting career. He achieved success, appearing on Broadway with George C. Scott in "Sly Fox," but began getting more voice work than stage work. That began a long and successful career that included recorded books, commercials, NFL documentaries, narrations at Disney's Epcot Center and Hershey Park, and the dangerous news voice in skits on *The Late Show* with David Letterman. His rich baritone provided the menacing narration for John Lurie's cult-classic *Fishing with John* series and the widely popular "Get rid of cable" DIRECTV commercials.

Despite embracing life in New York City and through all of his professional success as a disc jockey, actor, voice artist and photographer, Robb Webb maintained deep connections with Appalachia through his support of important cultural ventures such as Appalshop and *PMS&G*, as well as individual visual, literary, and performance artists. His influence on his younger brother became clearer to me when I learned that the tacky pink flamingos, such a big part of Jim's life, actually began with Robb, who gathered the first fake flock of sixteen Don Featherstone originals in the early 1980s at a department store in New York, juggling eight boxes of the plastic beauties through studios in Midtown to his Manhattan apartment before planting them at his home upstate.

While I had met Robb before, I got to know him mostly by telephone fifteen years ago during my graduate work on Jim and the editing of his book, *Get in, Jesus*. Robb was a candid, gracious and generous man who admired his brother. As we finished our phone interview, I asked him if I missed asking anything. "No," he said. "I just hope people see Jim as a hero for all he's done. In fact, he is my hero." Jim made the same comment about Robb many times over the years. We should all be so lucky.

Robb Webb died February 3, 2021 of complications from Covid-19. He left behind his wife of 30 years, Pat De Rousie-Webb, daughter Allison (Donald) Willcox, grandkids Michael and Sara Willcox, as well as a remarkable legacy of artistry in his photographs, voice work and legion of friends. A memorial to the Webb brothers is located in Whitesburg's Lewis Cemetery beside old US 119. They both left the "whirled" a better place.

Barto, Sally. "Letcher County's '60 Minutes' Man," *The Mountain Eagle*, Whitesburg, Kentucky. 5 August 2015.

Ward, Karla. "Ky. native Robb Webb has died. You may not know his name, but you probably know his voice." *Herald-Leader*, Lexington, Kentucky. 6 February 2021.

Webb's DirecTV commercials compilation: https://www.youtube.com/watch?v=NZ80SVOHKoo

Robb Webb

Farewell at Olana

Digital photograph

Randi Ward

Pitch Pine

So now
I'm *brave*
because
I stayed
and made
a stand?

You land
where
you land.

Seth Rosenbloom

From the Mouth
to the Most Distant Source

I am from low thick woods
pressed open by thumbs
of a river

who empties old rocks
of their luster
into creeks the color of coffee and cream.

The water, a hymn without end
runs east into the lap
of the bay

where sandpipers divine
soil from grains of salt.

Up west, worn
Appalachians shake
a thousand hands

with a sky stooped
too low to carry
a name.

Like the river,
I have no memory
of being born.

I awake, fireflies christen night
warm air buoys the skull.

Here, crickets rush
katydids seesaw
longing finds safe harbor.

And I know the heart
will always be a river.

Karl Plank

Echoing Impressions

In memory of Alene Clayton Holderby

The prayer cloths, you said, were for
whispering thoughts at night
that, when I no longer see wisps of scarf
in the sky, I might remember the earthy
petrichor that scents air before hard rain,
air that heavies ahead of downpour
and the soddening of wizened bones
only to lighten again as clouds
enfolding the knob of Black Balsam;
that in darkness I might say with the hush,
lift me, like mist rising on the mountain's peak,
before I vanish and am gone.

163

BOOK REVIEWS
&
NEWS

BOOK REVIEW by JIM CLARK

Valerie Nieman
To the Bones

(Morgantown, WV: West Virginia University Press, 2019)
204 pages; $19.99 paper.

I should probably admit a bias at the beginning of
this review. If one were to tailor a "favorite genre" for my
admittedly small and peculiar demographic, it might be
something like "Appalachian eco-horror mystery." When
my review copy of Valerie Nieman's novel *To the Bones*
arrived and I began reading, it quickly became clear that
it belongs to that tightly focused genre. There is definitely
some Poe lurking in the background, and certainly some
H.P. Lovecraft, as well as North Carolina practitioners like
Manly Wade Wellman and Fred Chappell. There might
even be a dash or two of Stephen King. All this is not to say
that Nieman is particularly derivative, but rather to place
this book in its proper genre and briefly trace its lineage.

The novel's hapless hero, Darrick MacBrehon, is a
federal auditor from Washington, D.C., driving through
West Virginia at night on his way home from a business
trip to Tennessee. Running low on gas, he pulls off the
interstate and stops at a forlorn convenience store. The
story opens gruesomely in medias res with Darrick waking
in a dark, dank, reeking mine pit with a gaping head
wound surrounded by what he discovers are human bones
and other less savory articles of decomposition. Through
a superhuman effort, he manages to hoist himself (using
a femur!) up the pit's slimy wall toward the glimmer of
daylight. Once out, he discovers he is on property belonging
to the Kavanagh Coal and Limestone Company. He makes

his way to a road and a sweepstakes parlor run by Lourana Taylor, a hard-bitten woman who has lived in Redbird, West Virginia, all her life.

Against her better judgment, Lourana offers the stinking, staggering (he's had episodic ataxia from childhood), wounded stranger food and shelter. Lourana's daughter, Dreama, who worked for the Kavanagh Company, has recently disappeared and Lourana has devoted herself to finding out what happened. She strongly suspects foul play by the powerful Kavanagh family—Patrick, the patriarch, and his two sons Eamon and Cormac. And while Darrick lost everything when he was attacked—wallet, car, cellphone—he discovers that his head injury has given him the ability to psychically "read" people's emotional states, which is useful in protecting himself.

Darrick and Lourana quickly become allies (and perhaps more) in determining why he was attacked and what happened to Dreama. Aided by a former deputy and a journalist investigating a toxic acid spill, they go up against the Kavanagh family. The Kavanaghs have ruled the county for generations and give the term "predatory capitalist" a whole new dimension of meaning. The tale concludes with a climactic confrontation, both physical and supernatural.

Nieman is a master of the unexpected twists and turns necessary for a page-turning mystery, and she deploys them in spare, poetic prose paced beautifully. She also possesses a deep knowledge and understanding of West Virginia, Appalachian culture, and the devastating effects of mining and renders them vitally and believably. There is some enjoyable satire when Darrick is sighted early on staggering down the road by a family who start a rumor about a "zombie" on the loose, which spreads like wildfire through the county, involving both the local religious community and law enforcement. More serious satire is afforded by the clever use of the Kavanaghs, who reputedly can "strip a man to the bone" (193), as a metaphor for the coal industry's exploitation of the land. Some fascinating Celtic lore is interwoven into the family's history and heritage. Parts of Dreama's story are potentially problematic plot-wise, and the book seems to hurry toward its conclusion, but neither compromises the success of the novel. All in all, *To the Bones* is compelling, satisfying, and well written.

BOOK REVIEW by KAREN GEORGE

Pauletta Hansel
Friend

(Loveland, OH: Dos Madres Press, 2020)
50 pages; $18, paper.

In the Foreword to *Friend*, Pauletta Hansel explains that her book originated in her "From Draft to Craft" poetry class where members wrote poems in the form of letters to other members. As the global pandemic intervened, she says the poems became "a source of creative and emotional strength and support as we navigated the new world in which we found ourselves" (ix).

The intimacy, tenderness, and vulnerability of these poems of direct address is what first drew me in. Though they each address a particular friend, it felt as if the poet also spoke to herself, me, and the world at large—which resulted in the powerful effect of making me feel at ease and deeply connected to what she observed, meditated on, and questioned.

The epistolary poems are titled with the dates they were written, from "March 16, 2020" to "June 17, 2020." The first poem opens with the intriguing question: "Friend, do you believe kindness / is enough?" (1). It ends with another weighty question: "Do you believe we'll learn / to take enough?" (1). The poem repeats the words "I want" and "wanting" six times—a yearning that creates tension which reverberates throughout the book, between wanting more and appreciating the abundance you already have.

Hansel weaves many of the poems by what she experiences during walks in cemeteries, along city sidewalks, or a bike trail along a river. The poems contain moments of the natural world's beauty and transformation. Messages of longing, connection, and hope left by others also appear in poems and photographs— *"I miss my fam"* (23) spray painted on a picnic table, a Tweety Bird chalked "on the cracked asphalt trail" (25), and "in the same yellow chalk, / fainter now, words fading into the path: / 'We will be OK'" (26).

The poems also speak of hurt, loss, aging, death, grief, and memory. She writes of a new grandbaby she's only seen virtually and how "All over the internet, daughters, sisters, wives / are locked outside the nursing home door. / The newspapers say those who die / are mostly dying alone" (3). There are haunting images of greed and violence— "purple waves of wanting— / the grocery shelves, picked clean. / A flock of turkey buzzards rises up, sated" (1)— which echo disturbing pictures we've seen on the news as the pandemic began: "the wildlife market, / the stacked cages, / claw and beak and blood-matted fur" (4). The interrelation of humans and the natural world threads throughout the book.

How timely the poems are—not only a record of pandemic times—but an archive of our ongoing connection and isolation as humans. Images of safety and comfort rub up against those of danger and uneasiness; yearning contrasts with gratitude as in the following humble admission:

> I'm telling you
> the hardest thing
> I've ever had to do
> is to stop wanting
> what I already have. (20)

The poems also reference the widespread summer protests and our country's history of social injustices, in lines such as "A flood is rising from the wounds / we've tried for centuries to ignore" (28).

At the book's center a longer, sectioned poem delves into blame and responsibility, weaving the history of invasive Bradford pear trees to the origins of the coronavirus and how we, as humans, alter and damage the environment without thought to how our actions return to haunt us.

Hansel layers the poems with images of life's dualities and mysteries. One poem uses the image of a racehorse "bred for the win's scent. / Those impossible legs like winged twigs / that will snap in a high wind" (20). She expresses this dualism of life regarding humans as well: "What moves us onward is the same, / sometimes, as what breaks us to the ground" (20).

Another important feature that braids these poems are moments of levity and wit, as when she refers to the "squirrels / who keep no distance / from our tulips and tomatoes" (5), "geese social distancing, / waddling away in their family units" (25) and how "a busted tire splayed open / looks just like a peacock feather Mardi Gras mask" (21).

These poems hum with openness, reverence, and compassion—as seen in the following lines that have stayed with me:

> We are all in the room, friend,
> no matter what door we entered.
> We call the room longing;
> we are in it together,
> alone. (22)

In the Foreword, Hansel states, "I found that direct address to beloved friends was how I could best speak my difficult truths" (ix-x). These clearheaded, breathtaking poems were just what I needed during these complex pandemic times—poems of comfort alongside uncomfortable truths about our human condition and the vital reminder that "there is no shadow / without light" (10).

BOOK REVIEW by CLHOE N. KINCART

Tina Parker
Lock Her Up

(Lexington, KY: Accents Publishing, 2021)
59 pages; $16.00 paper.

Lock Her Up, Tina Parker's third poetry collection, pierces a dark historical veil to expose the abuses of early 19th century women trapped at the Southwestern Lunatic Asylum, in the heart of Virginia. Parker draws on the medical design of "Admission, Treatment, and Release" and a confessional style to deliver disconsolate and marginalized voices of women once living in the hills where the poet herself grew up. Tuned to the impact of institutional discourse, tonal fragments, and white space, Parker twists historical experience into a poetic revelation.

Parker's fluid language blends with the rhetorical forms defining asylum practices: "Soon I'll hold / Her / Soon / Now it's only my knees / I cradle / And rock" (35). Individual poems replicate patient records, rules, letters, lists, and case studies. Others replicate the interpretations or traumatized responses of patients, bringing characters to life. Reading *Lock Her Up* is like digging through a filing cabinet of institutional secrets. For example, "Deposition" and "Patient Record" are inspired by original patient records conveying lived experiences through demographics and truncated ancillary data. Parker's manipulation of form invites readers to imagine the harsh reality of institutional oppression and discrimination, where women are tormented based on their distorted abnormality in a gender-oppressive culture. Such revelation is demonstrated in "The Incident: Noon":

(The Record said)   I struggle
                         And resisted
                         And ran my stomach

                              Into walls

(The Record said)   I screamed
                         I'd kill the baby
                         Or make myself go

                              Into labor

The Record said (33)

Slow rhythms and short lines in poems such as "Marriage" and "Deposition" match the solitary, inescapable, and consuming nature of the asylum, creating a coldly objective tone. Masterful use of enjambment pushes this coordination further, illuminating the distraught, pitiful, and deserted theme that follows each tragedy. The emotion pouring from line to line had me hanging onto every word, and the suspense throughout sews struggle together like a story.

Parker's incongruent pairings are depicted in "Tending the Baby": "There is no dementia / The doctor says / Only hysteria" (27). Here, "dementia" is misconstrued as "hysteria," displaying the institution's intentions to deceive and control. In the poem "Answered Letters," anger and insanity fall in close proximity, expanding the perceptions of how women patients are misdiagnosed, and thus incorrectly treated.

At times, Parker employs repetition to emphasize the broken state of her imprisoned speakers. The echoes in "Pleas for Release" reflect a trance-like state of false hope:

"My Son, will you arrange for my release / I was widowed at 40 and lost everything / Oh father, will you arrange for my release / I was betrayed by one who ought to have protected me…" (21). These refrains in the collection symbolize the women's ongoing struggle with social prejudice and their co-opted identities. Overall, the eerie echo provoked by enjambment and repetition lingers in the poem's words and structure, saturating the mind in darkness.

Lock Her Up delves into a forgotten world of torture and the damage and loss transpiring behind institutionally sanctioned walls. What emerges is a testimony to the lasting strength of women who cling to the remnants of a tarnished life. This inspirational collection demands that readers recognize women's resilient response to the systematic pollution that has had a sustaining and detrimental effect on their lives. These narratives remind us that impact and story may dwell beyond the public record or organized social discourse. By reimagining history, Parker creates a platform that exposes women's oppression and offers true reflection for the progressive future of gender equality.

BOOK REVIEW by THOMAS ALAN HOLMES

Kari Gunter-Seymour
A Place So Deep Inside America
It Can't Be Seen

(Russell, KY: Sheila-Na-Gig Editions, 2020)
64 pages; $16 paper.

A key to reading Kari Gunter-Seymour's *A Place So Deep Inside America It Can't Be Seen* occurs early, with the line "Everything alive aches for more" (17), because that assertion indicates why this collection requires repeated readings. To be sure, her book contains many expressions of hurt, such as surviving the difficult deaths of parents, coping with the loss of relationships as children's marriages fail, and enduring the melded trauma of isolation as societal and economic forces uproot sustaining tradition and family. At the same time, it addresses resilience as generations of women have confronted limitations of opportunity, proscribed roles, and genuine physical threat. In this volume, aching confirms life and asserts the need for hope.

The opening poem introduces these themes as an abrupt schism between old knowledge and new information: "Gone are the magics and songs, / all the things our grandmothers buried— . . . // inscribed by all who came before" (17), an acknowledgment of legacy and tradition in the acts of survival later described as "signs / of consequence, the significance / long lost to me with many mountain ways" (20).

These poems acknowledge that the cycles of planting and regrowth contend with social and economic conventions, both in turn tied to violence. In "When You

Meet My Mother," the speaker prompts, "Ask her how poor can sink a body as good as rocks in a river. / . . . Ask her how poverty, with hot breath, / sneaks up from behind, holds you down in the barn" (19). When the speaker of "Pack Horse Librarians" later states, "Only women of disrepute were considered / working women by the church" (23), we begin to recognize the many reasons why such actions and such people "can't be seen"—they are elements of lost knowledge; they are secret violences disputed in the face of open accusation; they are unsanctioned ways of life not to be tolerated. The poems challenge the notion of how the disconnection between the natural world and the spirit conditions us to be incapable of recognizing the life immediately before us. However, Gunter-Seymour shows how women of spirit adapt, offering a direct heroic lineage from the granny women to the pack librarians to the munitions workers to the trapped mother who "always seemed to make choices / that were not so much decision / as the least worst option" (46), if only to follow a tragic trajectory against overwhelming forces, aching for more.

Men are almost completely absent from this volume, although their influence pervades it. We see the effects of powerful men to whom the communities depicted would remain unseen. In "Planting by the Signs," the speaker draws a stark contrast between her nature-attuned grandmother and the disparaging billionaire Mike Bloomberg, who claimed he "could teach anybody to be a farmer" (51). In "If My Mama Had Fallen for Jim Jones," the speaker offers the bitter suggestion that the quick and fearful death of being a part of that cult would have been more merciful than the prolonged, frustrated hopes exploited by the televangelist Jimmy Swaggart and his ilk. Even Hank Williams, the favorite singer of a father present mostly in his dying, could not endure the injury and despair the beloved father has suffered. These real men known by the speakers offer only fleeting joy. In "Hold Fast," we learn of a father "fresh from the war, / metaled and wired, a great catch" for her mother, a father further broken down by his best option for earning a living in the coal mines. Still, he has encouraged his daughter to sing the Hank songs, the poignancy of the shared music growing stronger as the adult daughter understands its underpinnings (43). An earlier poem offers an expected plan as wife: ". . . my job was to stay clean and thankful, / mostly invisible, as though telling me what to do / told me who I was" (21). In "Wedding Dress," the speaker declares herself a "freewoman" seeing her younger self as an actor in a marriage, "that girl / stunningly unacquainted with loss" whom her despised wedding dress represents: "I wanted to drown / the bitch" (33). That loss of love resonates throughout, the speaker in "To the Bone" whispering a name as the season turns cold, the speaker in "Once I Had Wings" stating, "I have grown to crave even your silence" (45).

Even after a family history of neglectful husbands, abusive cousins and uncles, and a careful attempt to raise a son transcending those patriarchal wrongful prerogatives, "the brave heart my son had been, / the farm boy, the quipster, / the *Ren & Stimpy* imitator" (27), the speaker finds her son damaged by war just as her father has been, his PTSD altering the course of his promising life, destroying his marriage, and creating a rift between the speaker and a beloved granddaughter who "might never make out why / her body aches for seed and trowel" (41). One cannot miss the pervasive image of uprootedness as Gunter-Seymour explores it in so many literal and figurative senses.

Rich in sensory images, filled with music, Gunter-Seymour's *A Place So Deep* offers a moving recognition of the losses suffered in our current accelerated generational shifts. It nevertheless offers an assertive fortitude, moving from a persona describing herself as "words piled a hundred apologies deep" (20) to one who cherishes "a trickle of grace, / our uneasy peace unwilling to unknot" (54). In this collection, Gunter-Seymour encourages us to nurture that peace like a seed.

NEW BOOKS

LINDA PARSONS

Support your regional authors!

An ongoing feature of *Pine Mountain Sand & Gravel* is an annual listing of recent book titles and publishers' blurbs from past and present contributors.

Crimson Sunshine: Reflections with Poetry & Prose is an introduction to **Jessica Weyer Bentley**'s poetry that stems from a life lived with great lows and ultimate highs as seen through the eyes of both a 5-year-old girl and survivor of astounding loss and her accomplished mother. Illustrated by Laura Bentley (AlyBlue Media, 2020).

My Mother's Red Ford: New and Selected Poems (1986-2020) represents **Roy Bentley**'s first six award-winning books. Kate Fox writes, "Readers of the Dayton, Ohio, native's previous collections will recognize many of the people and places …All are elevated through the loving crucible of memory and language to divine status" (Work Horse Press, 2020).

Ace Boggess' *Escape Envy,* writes Francesca Bell, "is a book of reckoning, a poetry collection that takes clear-eyed but tender measure of what we lose when we lose ourselves—to addiction, heartache, incarceration, and to time's ravenous passage" (Brick Road Poetry Press, 2021).

Noah Davis' stunning debut collection, *Of This River,* ushers in a new era of poems from the Allegheny region of Appalachia. This soulful meditation on a neglected region of America reveals a legacy of lingering violence to land and animal alike. Striking stories and scenes portray the spiritual cost of deep poverty, the necessity to ask for forgiveness, and the joy in praising the beauty still found in the steep hollows (Wheelbarrow Books, 2020).

Mary Lucille DeBerry's third poetry collection, *She Was the Girl* (Sarvis Press, 2020), "constitutes a journey back into the childhood of a West Virginia girl, a keen observer of the scene; then forward into our politically dark days...," writes Norman Julian. Of DeBerry's first collection, *Bertha Butcher's Coat* (Revised Edition, Sarvis Press, 2020), Lori Wilson writes, "These are poems that remind us of our roots even as they reckon with the change that inevitably comes." The recent books join *Alice Saw the Beauty* to form a trilogy.

Victor Depta's *Where to Run, Where to Hide*, and *The Temple of Scattered Lives* comprise Volume 2 of his mystery series, *What They Yearn For*. Set in hilly Kentucky and San Francisco, they involve college professors, the Middle East, devil worship, and an Asian nursery (Blair Mountain Press, 2021).

"Art makes life's events presentable and almost bearable," notes Shelby Stephenson. "**Nancy Dillingham**'s *I Can't Breathe* holds that reality in Fate's recognition, plus the promise that living breathes and cries for space and breadth" (Kelsay Books, 2021).

Jane Ann Fuller's *Half-Life* spans the years of coming to terms with the suicide of a husband and its traumatic effect on the children: drug abuse, rape, unflinching self-analysis, survivor's guilt. These poems look to the self but also outward, to the healing physical world (Sheila-Na-Gig Editions, 2021).

Pauletta Hansel's eighth poetry collection is *Friend*, epistolary poems written in the early days of the pandemic. Richard Hague writes, "…it is a caring testimony to absent friends and family, to a loyal husband, to the rejuvenative powers of nature, even in the city, and a grudging paean to walking" (Dos Madres Press, 2020).

Of **Randel McCraw Helms**' collection, *Animal Prayers*, Devon Balwit writes, "The poet calls the Anthropocene to account—our polluting, our hunting, our meddling destruction of habitat—but in language so rich and tender that even as we are guilt-ridden, we are mysteriously joyful" (Kelsay Books, 2020).

"What more can we ask of a poet than to pull back the curtain, lay bare a collective heart?" asks Natalie Sypolt. "**Stephanie Kendrick** does this for us with *The Places We Feel Warm*. This chapbook shows the complex and fierce Appalachian woman—the mother and partner, the broken and battered, the mended. The soaring. The vulnerable badass" (Main Street Rag Publishing, 2021).

Jeff Mann's new poetry collection, *Redneck Bouquet,* has the poet seeking out sweet donuts and bringing home a lonely man, shucking flannels and boots. His poems are grounded in West Virginia's mountains, his adoration for the region's culture, and the frisson of passion between men. These verses reflect the commonplace and concupiscent joys of rural America (Lethe Press, 2020).

Of **Wendy McVicker**'s new chapbook, *Zero, a Door,* Pauletta Hansel writes, "McVicker sees with an artist's eye and listens with the ear of a poet to what the world speaks to us, the grasses with their 'wind-brushed hiss / a kind of silence'" (The Orchard Street Press, 2021).

Through 30 surviving letters of Sergeant John M. Douhit to his wife, **Elaine Fowler Palencia**'s *On Rising Ground: The Life and Civil War Letters of John M. Douthit, 52nd Georgia Volunteer Infantry Regiment* presents, as W. Clifford Roberts Jr. writes, "a poignant account of a Confederate foot soldier from the mountains of North Georgia." Palencia is a descendant of Douhit's (Mercer University Press, 2021).

Tina Parker's third poetry collection, *Lock Her Up*, gives voice to the women from the not-too- distant past who were not allowed to make decisions about their own bodies and mental health. In this thought-provoking collection, Parker brings to life three characters and highlights their stories through poems and research (Accents Publishing, 2021).

Karl Plank's *The Fact of the Cage: Reading and Redemption in David Foster Wallace's Infinite Jest* shows how Wallace's masterpiece dramatizes the condition of encagement and how it comes to be met by "Abiding" and through interrelational acts of speaking and hearing, touching, and facing (Routledge, 2021).

In **Sarah Pross**' debut chapbook, *Grounding*, Sue Weaver Dunlap writes that Pross "shares her rooted landscape in the Southern Appalachian Mountains in these poems, formed from 'a bundle of the unwritten/wrapped in human skin about nature, ancestors, and faith …from her 'dead people box' that are all very much alive" (Main Street Rag Publishing, 2021).

Of *The Distance Beyond Sight*, Anne Marie Macari writes, "**Susan Sailer**'s distilled, powerful poems are written against the American narrative of the happy family. This poet is that feared thing—a truth-teller. From the suffering of the natural world to the desperation of refugees, Sailer keeps an unrelenting focus. The world isn't ordered or just, but it is cherished" (Main Street Rag Publishing, 2020).

The Land of the Dead Is Open for Business is an extended elegy for **Jacob Strautmann**'s home state of West Virginia and its generations of inhabitants sold out by the false promise of the American Dream. Voices rise up from the page to describe a landscape eroded and plundered by runaway capitalism (Four Way Books, 2020).

In *Arranging Deck Chairs on the Titanic*, **Mike Wilson** "distills our anger with skill and wit," writes Sherry Chandler, as he "guides us through this upside-down world where 'Antarctica is hotter than L.A.' and 'all the answers on Jeopardy are lies.' Such arrangement …might be an assertion of human dignity in the face of madness" (Rabbit House Press, 2020).

Amy Wright's *Paper Concert: A Conversation in the Round* weaves a decades-plus questions and answers from a range of discussions the author has had with artists, activists, scientists, philosophers, physicians, priests, musicians, and others who refract the light of the unknowable mystery of the self (Sarabande Books, 2021).

CONTRIBUTORS

Elizabeth Bailey spent the first twenty years of her career as a journalist, ten years as a family therapist, and is most recently working on poems. She is a 2019 MFA graduate in poetry at the Writing Seminars at Bennington College.

Courtney Barnoski grew up in Happy Hollow in Lewis County, Kentucky. She is a graduate of Thomas More University, with a BA in English/creative writing. Courtney is known for themes of social justice, mental health awareness, and trauma. In her spare time, she grabs her camera and heads for the woods, looking for little moments to freeze in time.

Diana Becket was born in Manchester, England, and lived in the Netherlands before moving to Ohio. She began to write poetry when she retired from teaching composition courses at the University of Cincinnati. She writes in a cabin on the Ohio River. Her poems have appeared in *Common Threads, The Cape Rock*, and *Muddy River Poetry Review.*

Gaby Bedetti is professor of English at Eastern Kentucky University. Her poems, photos, and translations have appeared in *Cold Mountain Review, Typehouse*, and *World Literature Today.* She is assembling a co-translation of the poems of Henri Meschonnic.

Jessica Weyer Bentley's first collection of poetry, *Crimson Sunshine*, was published in 2020 (AlyBlue Media). Jessica is a contributing writer for the award-winning series, *Grief Diaries*. Her work is anthologized in the 2020 Women of Appalachia Project, *Women Speak* Vol. 6 and in the Ohio Poetry Association's 2020 *Common Threads*, and a pandemic poem appeared in *Global Poemic*. Jessica resides with her husband and two children in northwest Ohio.

Roy Bentley, a finalist for the 2018 Miller Williams prize for *Walking with Eve in the Loved City*, has published eight books, including *American Loneliness* and *My Mother's Red Ford: New & Selected Poems* from Lost Horse Press. He received a Creative Writing Fellowship from the NEA and fellowships from the Florida Division of Cultural Affairs and Ohio Arts Council. *Hillbilly Guilt* won the 2019 Hidden River Arts/Willow Run Poetry Book Award.

Robert Beveridge makes noise (xterminal.bandcamp.com) and writes poetry in Akron, Ohio. Poems have appeared or are forthcoming in *cattails, ellipsis...*, and *Ample Remains*, among others.

Michelle Boettcher is a creative writer, photographer, and faculty member at Clemson University. She engages in a variety of projects that overlap with the work of the Appalachian Studies Association. This is her first submission to *Pine Mountain Sand & Gravel*.

Ace Boggess is author of six books of poetry, most recently *Escape Envy* (Brick Road Poetry Press, 2021). His writing has appeared in *Michigan Quarterly Review, Notre Dame Review, Mid-American Review, River Styx*, and others. He received a fellowship from the West Virginia Commission on the Arts and spent five years in a West Virginia prison. He lives in Charleston, WV.

Joyce Compton Brown is a Pushcart Prize nominee and author of three poetry collections, *Bequest* (Finishing Line), *Singing with Jarred Edges* (Main Street Rag), and the forthcoming *Standing on the Outcrop* (Redhawk Publications). She has published in *Broadkill Review*, *The Blue Mountain Review*, and *Kakalak*, among others. She enjoys hanging out on Linville Mountain and holding the cat.

A retired biologist, **Les Brown** is a native of the North Carolina Mountains. A Pushcart nominee, he has published in *Pinesong*, *Front Porch Review*, *Flying South*, *Kakalak*, *Avalon*, and others. His book, *A Place Where Trees Had Names*, was published in 2020 by Redhawk Publications. Les lives with his wife, Joyce, in Troutman, NC.

The sculptor **Julie Byrne** lives with her husband in an 1800s brick farmhouse on property that abuts the old Ohio Canal. As an Ohio Arts Council artist, she works at Groveport Madison High School and is working with that community on an outdoor tile mural based on Amanda Gorman's poem "The Hill We Climb." Julie maintains a clay studio in Columbus and operates a paint-your-own pottery business there.

Pam Campbell is a daughter of the Appalachian Mountains. Her work as a clinical social worker, community organizer, and teacher informs her writing. She favors the songlike qualities of poetic form and how form serves to contain human suffering and joy. Her poems have appeared in *Ó Bhéal Five Words Vol XIV Anthology*.

Sam Campbell is a writer and teacher from Tennessee. She is the fiction editor and co-founder of *Black Moon*. She publishes across all genres; her work appears in *October Hill* and *Tennessee's Emerging Poets Anthology*, among others. Awards include the James Still Prize for Short Fiction and the Jesse Stuart Prize for YA Writing, among others.

Jim Clark is professor emeritus of English at Barton College in Wilson, North Carolina. His books include *Notions: A Jim Clark Miscellany*; two collections of poetry, *Dancing on Canaan's Ruins* and *Handiwork*; and he edited *Fable in the Blood: The Selected Poems of Byron Herbert Reece*.

Greg Clary's poems have appeared in *The Rye Whiskey Review*, *North/South Appalachia*, *The Watershed Journal*, and others, with photographs in *The Sun*, *Tiny Seed Literary Journal*, *Dark Horse*, among others. *Piercing the Veil: Appalachian Visions*, with Byron Hoot, contains photo ekphrastic poems (Amazon Publishing, 2020). Greg is professor emeritus of rehab and human services at Clarion University in Pennsylvania.

Rita Coleman resides in rural Greene County, Ohio, with her husband the scientist, a dog, a cat, and a rabbit. Her poetry books include *And Yet* (2017) and *Mystic Connections* (2009), and she has a BA and MA in English literature from Wright State University. She's not sure if she's the laziest poet around, but she may be the laziest poet she knows.

Carson Colenbaugh is a student of horticulture and forestry at Clemson University, with publications in *Canary* and Clemson's journal, *The Chronicle*. He was selected as a student poet for Southern Wesleyan University's annual literary festival in 2021 and 2020 and for Clemson's Writers' Harvest event in 2019. He lives and works around the Blue Ridge Escarpment.

Jessica Cory is from southeastern Ohio but lives in western NC where she teaches in the English department at Western Carolina University. She's the editor of *Mountains Piled upon Mountains: Appalachian Nature Writing in the Anthropocene* (WVU Press, 2019), and her work has appeared in *Still: The Journal, ellipsis…*, and *Menacing Hedge¸* among others.

Owen Cramer is not a poet or an Appalachian. He is, however, married to Pauletta Hansel who is both, so something was bound to rub off on him, eventually. His only other published poem appeared in *PMS&G* Volume 13 (Vultures) and was reprinted in *Quarried: Three Decades of Pine Mountain Sand & Gravel.*

Noah Davis was raised in Tipton, Pennsylvania, and writes about the Allegheny Front. *Of This River* won the 2019 Wheelbarrow Emerging Poet Book Prize from Michigan State University. He has published in *The Sun, Orion, North American Review, Atlanta Review*, and others. Noah was a Katharine Bakeless Nason Fellow at the Bread Loaf Writers' Conference and received the 2018 Jean Ritchie Appalachian Literature Fellowship from Lincoln Memorial University.

Victor M. Depta is the publisher of Blair Mountain Press, established in 1999, with a focus on the environment of Appalachia. Dr. Depta has published eleven books of poetry, four novels, two volumes of comedic plays, two collections of essays on poetry and mysticism, a memoir, and poems in magazines and journals.

Timothy Dodd is from Mink Shoals, West Virginia, and the author of *Fissures, and Other Stories* (Bottom Dog Press, 2019). His stories have appeared in *Yemassee, Broad River Review, Anthology of Appalachian Writers, Crab Creek Review, Roanoke Review*, and elsewhere.

Hilda Downer lives in Sugar Grove, North Carolina, and is a longtime member of SAWC. She has published in numerous journals and anthologies. Her book of poetry, *When Light Waits For Us*, is forthcoming from Main Street Rag Publishing. She is retired from teaching English at Appalachian State University and from psychiatric nursing.

Sue Weaver Dunlap grew up East Tennessee and lives near Walland, Tennessee, on a mountain farm. Here, she writes poetry, fiction, and memoir. She has a chapbook, *The Story Tender* (Finishing Line Press, 2014), and a full collection, *Knead* (Main Street Rag, 2016). *A Walk to the Spring House* is forthcoming from Iris Press.

Jane Ann Fuller, recipient of the James Boatwright III Poetry Prize, is a descendent of riverboat gamblers and horse thieves and was born and raised in Hocking County, Ohio. Her work appears in *Shenandoah, Still: The Journal, Northern Appalachia Review, The MacGuffin, The American*

Journal of Poetry, and elsewhere. *Half-Life* was published by Sheila-Na-Gig Editions in 2021.

Vanda Galen was born in Big Woods, Kentucky, grew up in Morehead, and has lived in exile for over 40 years in the upper Midwest, where she was a professor and department chair in social work until retiring in 2012. Yearly visits to family, Hindman Settlement School, and Sheltowee Trace keep her connected to her culture. Her photography documents her world travels and trips back home.

Michael Garrigan's essays and poems have appeared in *The Drake Magazine, Gray's Sporting Journal, Split Rock Review,* and *Permafrost*. His chapbook, *What I Know [How to Do]*, is available from Finishing Line Press, and his first full-length collection, *Robbing the Pillars*, was published by Homebound Publications in 2020.

Karen George is the author of five chapbooks and two collections from Dos Madres Press: *Swim Your Way Back* (2014) and *A Map and One Year* (2018), with work in *Adirondack Review, Valparaiso Poetry Review, Salamander, Main Street Rag,* and *Poet Lore*. She reviews poetry at http://readwritepoetry.blogspot.com/. https://karenlgeorge.blogspot.com/

Scott Goebel is a writer, editor, and gypsy scholar. His work has appeared in *Appalachian Journal, Cold Mountain Review, Iron Mountain Review, Wind Magazine, Journal of Kentucky Studies,* and *Now & Then*. He edited Jim Webb's *Get In, Jesus* (Wind, 2012) and Joe Barrett's *Blue Planet Memoirs* (Dos Madres, 2018) and is an editor emeritus of this journal.

Connie Jordan Green lives on a farm in East Tennessee, where she writes and gardens. She is the author of two award-winning novels for young people, two poetry chapbooks, and two poetry collections, most recently *Darwin's Breath* from Iris Press. Her poetry has appeared in numerous anthologies and journals and has been nominated for Pushcart Prizes.

Joanne Greenway grew up in rural New York State and has lived in Cincinnati since 1972. A retired social worker, her work has been anthologized in numerous publications. She has two chapbooks, both by Finishing Line Press: *Limited Engagement* (2016) and *True Confessions* (2019). She serves as president of the Greater Cincinnati Writers League.

Kari Gunter-Seymour's work was selected by former U.S. Poet Laureate Natasha Trethewey to be included in the PBS American Portrait crowdsourced poem, *Remix: For My People*. Her poems appear in numerous journals, including *Verse Daily, Rattle,* and *The NY Times*. She is the 2020 Ohio Poet of the Year and Poet Laureate of Ohio. www.karigunterseymourpoet.com

Richard Hague's latest collection, *Studied Days: Poems Early and Late in Appalachia* (Dos Madres Press, 2019), received Honorable Mention in The Writers Conference of Northern Appalachia's first book awards.

Catherine Hamrick is the copywriter for a liberal arts college in North Georgia. She has held editorial positions at *Better Homes and Gardens, Cooking Light, Southern Accents*, and Meredith Books. Poems have appeared in *The Blue*

Mountain Review, storySouth, Tiny Seed Literary Journal, Braided Way, The Ekphrastic Review, and elsewhere.

Pauletta Hansel's eighth poetry collection is *Friend,* epistolary poems written in the early days of the pandemic. Her writing has been featured in *Oxford American, Rattle, Appalachian Journal, Still: The Journal,* and *New Verse News,* among others. Pauletta was Cincinnati's first Poet Laureate (2016-2018) and is past managing editor of *Pine Mountain Sand & Gravel,* the journal of the Southern Appalachian Writers Cooperative. https://paulettahansel.wordpress.com/

Marc Harshman's poetry collection, *Woman in Red Anorak,* won 2017 Blue Lynx Prize. His 14th children's book, *Fallingwater,* co-author Anna Smucker, was published by Roaring Brook/Macmillan. He is co-winner of the 2019 Allen Ginsberg Poetry Award and the poet laureate of West Virginia.

Randel McCraw Helms is retired from Arizona State University's English department. Poems have recently appeared in *Dappled Things, Blood & Bourbon,* and *Silkworm.* His chapbook, *Animal Prayers,* was published last year by Kelsay Books.

Melissa Helton lives, writes, and teaches in southeast Kentucky. Her work has appeared or is forthcoming in *Anthology of Appalachian Writers, Shenandoah, Appalachian Review, Still: The Journal,* and more. Her chapbooks include *Inertia: A Study* (Finishing Line Press, 2016) and *Forward Through the Interval,* forthcoming from Workhorse.

Michael Henson is a former co-editor of *Pine Mountain Sand & Gravel. Maggie Boylan*, his prize-winning book of collected stories, came out in 2018 from Ohio University Press. *Secure the Shadow,* a novel, is forthcoming in 2021.

A native of upper East Tennessee, **Jane Hicks** is an award-winning poet, teacher, and quilter. Her poetry appears in *Still: The Journal, Appalachian Heritage, Shenandoah*, and *Asheville Poetry Review.* Her latest poetry collection, *Driving with the Dead* (University Press of Kentucky, 2014), won the Appalachian Writers Association Poetry Book of the Year Award and was a finalist for the Weatherford Award.

Ali Hintz is a queer Appalachian poet and farmer. Her work has appeared in *Miracle Monocle Anthology Series* and more. She is the book reviews editor for the *Arkansas International* and an MFA candidate at the University of Arkansas.

Pamela Hirschler grew up in eastern Kentucky, studied creative writing at Morehead State University, and received an MFA in poetry from Drew University. Her poetry and reviews have appeared in *Still: The Journal, Tupelo Quarterly,* and other journals. Her first poetry chapbook is *What Lies Beneath* (Finishing Line Press, 2019).

Thomas Alan Holmes teaches literature at East Tennessee State University. His work has appeared in such journals as *Valparaiso Poetry Review, Still: The Journal, Appalachian Journal, The Connecticut Review*, and *Appalachian Heritage*. His debut poetry collection, *In the Backhoe's Shadow*, is forthcoming from Iris Press.

Byron Hoot was born and raised in Morgantown, West Virginia, and resides in the Pennsylvania Wilds. Poems have recently appeared in *The Watershed Journal, Tobeco Literary Arts Journal, Adelaide*, and *Pennessence*. He is a co-founder of The Tamarack Writers (1974) and The Fernwood Writers Retreat (2019). Hootnhowlpoetry.com

Scott T. Hutchinson's work has appeared in *Appalachian Heritage, Yemassee, The Georgia Review*, and *The Southern Review*. New work is forthcoming in *Concho River Review, Aethlon, Soundings East, Steam Ticket, Cider Press Review*, and *Tar River Poetry*.

Stephanie Kendrick's first chapbook is *Places We Feel Warm* (Main Street Rag). Poems have appeared in *Sheila-Na-Gig Online*, Women of Appalachia Project's *Women Speak* Volumes 4, 5, and 6, *Ghost City Review, Northern Appalachia Review*, and in the collection *Not Far from Me: Stories of Opioids and Ohio*. stephthepoet.org

Clyde Kessler lives in Radford, Virginia, with his wife, Kendall, and their son, Alan. He has published poems in many magazines over the years, most recently in *Mad Swirl* and *Spinoza Blue*.

Clhoe N. Kincart resides in Northern Kentucky, attending Thomas More University in the law and English programs, with a creative writing concentration. Her award-winning poem, "Recipe for Fall," is in the university's 2020 issue of *Words*. As a multiple honor society member, student tutor, and server, Clhoe embraces challenge.

Patsy Kisner's poems have appeared in journals such as *Appalachian Journal, Shelia-Na-Gig, Modern Haiku,* and *Spoon River Poetry Review*. She has a poetry chapbook, *Inside the Horse's Eye,* and a poetry collection, *Last Days of an Old Dog,* both from Finishing Line Press.

Jordan Laney is an educator, writer, research consultant, and yoga instructor working in central Appalachia. She holds a PhD in cultural and social theory from Virginia Tech. Her writing can be found in *Dinner Bell* and *Bluegrass Unlimited.* www.jordanlaney.com

Chiquita Mullins Lee lives in Columbus and works for the Ohio Arts Council. A Pushcart Prize nominee, her nonfiction and fiction have appeared in *Poetry in the Time of Coronavirus,* among others, with work is featured on the PBS American Portrait project. Chiquita performs with Wild Women Writing and leads Word Warriors at New Covenant Believers Church.

Steven T. Licardi is a social worker, spoken word poet, and performance activist in southwest Virginia. Much of his work is at the intersections of mental health and civic systems of oppression. His poetry collection is *a billion burning dreams,* with work in *Latexo Beat, I Want You to See This Before I Leave, Xanadu,* and *Perspectives: Poetry Concerning Autism and Other Disabilities* (Volume II), among others.

Jimmy Long's poems have appeared in *Appalachian Review, Still: The Journal,* and *Kestrel,* among others, with work forthcoming in *Northern Appalachia Review* and *Presence:*

A Journal of Catholic Poetry. A native of Buckhannon, West Virginia, he works and lives in Charleston with his family of five.

Flavian Mark Lupinetti, a writer and cardiothoracic surgeon, obtained his MFA in writing from the Vermont College of Fine Arts. Stories and poems have appeared in *About Place, Barrelhouse, Bellevue Literary Review, Briar Cliff Review, Cutthroat, The Examined Life, Neon, Red Rock Review,* and *ZYZZYVA.*

Jeff Mann has published three poetry chapbooks, six full-length books of poetry, three collections of personal essays, a volume of memoir and poetry, three novellas, six novels, and three collections of short fiction. With Julia Watts, he co-edited *LGBTQ Fiction and Poetry from Appalachia.* The winner of two Lambda Literary Awards, he teaches creative writing at Virginia Tech.

John C. Mannone, a retired physicist in Knoxville, Tennessee, has poems in *North Dakota Quarterly, Le Menteur, Poetry South,* and others. A Jean Ritchie Fellowship winner in Appalachian literature (2017), he served as celebrity judge for the NFSPS (2018). His poetry won the Impressions of Appalachia Creative Arts Contest (2020). He edits poetry for *Abyss & Apex* and other journals.

Llewellyn McKernan has an MA in writing from Brown University. She has authored six poetry books for adults and four for children, with poems published in many journals and anthologies. Her work has won awards in state, regional, and national contests. Appalachia is her home because writing poems is "always home" to her, and she's written more poetry there than anywhere on earth.

Wendy McVicker is poet laureate of Athens, Ohio, and a longtime teaching artist. Her chapbook, *the dancer's notes* (Finishing Line Press) came out in 2015, and *Zero, a Door* is forthcoming from Orchard Street Press. She collaborates with musicians, dancers, and visual artists and performs with instrumentalist Emily Prince, under the name *another language altogether.*

Marianne Mersereau grew up along Virginia's Crooked Road in the southwest corner of the state. She is the author of the chapbook, *Timbrel* (Finishing Line Press, 2013). Her writing has appeared in *The Hollins Critic, Entropy, The Dead Mule School of Southern Literature, Still: The Journal, Point Arts Quarterly, Deep South Magazine*, and elsewhere.

Jim Minick is the author of five books, most recently, *Fire Is Your Water,* a novel. *The Blueberry Years,* his memoir, won the Best Nonfiction Book of the Year from Southern Independent Booksellers Association. Work has appeared in *The New York Times, Poets & Writers, Tampa Review, Shenandoah, Orion, Oxford American,* and *The Sun,* among others.

Deni Naffziger lives in Athens, Ohio. Her work has been published in *The New Ohio Review, Atticus Review, Spoon River,* and *Pikeville Review,* with work forthcoming in *Pudding Magazine* and *Northern Appalachian Review.* Her first full-length collection, *Desire to Stay,* was published by Stockport Flats Press.

Valerie Nieman was a journalist and farmer in West Virginia, then became a college professor in North Carolina. Her fourth novel, *To the Bones*, came out in 2019 from WVU Press. Her poetry has appeared in three collections, many anthologies, and journals from *The Georgia Review* to *Crannóg*.

Thomas Alan Orr has published two collections, *Hammers in the Fog* and *Tongue to the Anvil: New and Selected Poems*. Poems have appeared in the anthologies *Good Poems* (edited by Garrison Keillor), *In Whatever Houses We May Visit: Poems That Have Inspired Physicians,* and *In Praise of Fertile Land.*

Elaine Fowler Palencia's latest book is *On Rising Ground: The Life and Civil War Letters of John M. Douthit, 52ⁿᵈ Georgia Volunteer Infantry Regiment* (Mercer University Press, 2021). Recent poetry publications include *English Journal, Modern Mountain Magazine,* and *Hummingbird*. From Morehead, Kentucky, she lives in Champaign, Illinois.

Lisa Parker is a native Virginian, poet, musician, and photographer. Her book, *This Gone Place,* won the 2010 Appalachian Studies Association's Weatherford Award, and her work is widely published. Her photography has been exhibited in NYC and published in arts journals and anthologies.

Tina Parker is the author of three books of poetry. Her debut collection *Mother May I,* was published by Sibling Rivalry Press in 2016. Her newest book, *Lock Her Up,* is published by Accents Publishing. Tina grew up in Bristol,

Virginia, and now lives in Berea, Kentucky. She is a member of the Women of Appalachia Project.

Poet, playwright, and editor, **Linda Parsons** is the poetry editor for Madville Publishing and reviews editor for *Pine Mountain Sand & Gravel*. She is also copy editor for *Chapter 16,* the literary website of Humanities Tennessee. Widely published, her fifth poetry collection is *Candescent* (Iris Press, 2019). With this volume of *PMS&G*, she ends her tenure as reviews editor after five years. It was a great honor and pleasure, and she will continue to assist the next editor.

Rachel Anne Parsons is a queer Appalachian farmer, writer, and poet living in Olive Hill, Kentucky, where she helps to run a sustainable family homestead. She received her BA in English from East Tennessee State University, where she minored in Japanese, with an MFA in creative writing through the Bluegrass Writers Studio at Eastern Kentucky University.

Chrissie Anderson Peters is a native of Tazewell, Virginia. She lives in Bristol, Tennessee, with her husband and their four feline children. A graduate of Emory & Henry College and the University of Tennessee, she has written three books (*Dog Days and Dragonflies*, *Running From Crazy*, and *Blue Ridge Christmas*). Her passions include music (especially 80's) and travel. www.CAPWrites.com

Walt Peterson's poem in this volume represents a collaboration with the sculptor James Shipman. Walt lived with Shipman's sculpture (let's call her "Tish") for about a month before she consented to tell her tale to the poet. He lived with nine other sculptures by Shipman, and James lived with ten of Walt's poems. Their interpretation of each other's work comprised a show and reading at Seton Hill University.

Rhonda Pettit is professor of English and editor of *Blue Ash Review* at the University of Cincinnati Blue Ash College. She is the author of *Riding the Wave Train* (Dos Madres Press, 2017), *The Global Lovers* (2010 Cincinnati Fringe Festival), *Fetal Waters* (Finishing Line Press, 2013), and literary criticism on the work of Dorothy Parker. Poems were published recently in *Cold Mountain Review* and the *Anthology of Appalachian Writers*, Volume XII.

Karl Plank is the author of three books, most recently *The Fact of the Cage: Reading and Redemption in David Foster Wallace's Infinite Jest* (Routledge, 2021). Poetry has appeared in *Beloit Poetry Journal, Zone 3,* and *New Madrid,* among others. A winner of *Shenandoah*'s Thomas Carter Prize and a Pushcart nominee, he is the J.W. Cannon Professor of Religion at Davidson College.

Dale Marie Prenatt is from southern West Virginia by way of east Kentucky. She earned a BA in theatre from Morehead State. Poems have appeared in *Appalachian Reckoning: A Region Responds to Hillbilly Elegy* and *Quarried: Three Decades of Pine Mountain Sand & Gravel.* She works as a bookseller and lives in Cincinnati.

Sarah Pross was born, raised, and still resides in Seymour, Tennessee, with her rescue pup Charley. She has a BA in English literature from Maryville College. Poems have appeared in *Kakalak* and *Cathexis Northwest.* Sarah is the author of *Grounding* (Main Street Rag Publishing, 2020).

Bonnie Proudfoot's first novel, *Goshen Road,* published by Swallow Press in 2020, was selected by the Women's National Book Association for one of its 2020 Great Group Reads. It was also longlisted for the PEN/Hemingway award. Bonnie teaches English composition part-time for West Virginia University, and when the spirit moves her, works on glass art in her Athens, Ohio, studio.

Erin Miller Reid is a dermatologist living in Kingsport, Tennessee. Poems and fiction have been published in *Still: The Journal*, where her short story, "The Offering," won the 2018 fiction contest. Her fiction was also included in the Women of Appalachia Project's annual anthology, *Women Speak*, and is forthcoming in *Appalachian Review*. She is writing her first novel.

Kirsten Reneau received her MFA in creative nonfiction at the University of New Orleans. A Pushcart Prize nominee, her work can be seen in *The Threepenny Review, Hippocampus Magazine, Alaska Quarterly Review*, and others.

Kevin Rippin lives and writes in Greensboro, North Carolina. He has published articles, reviews, poetry, and fiction. His full-length poetry collection, *Amber Drive*, was published by Main Street Rag Press in 2018. Poems have appeared in *Poems from the Heron Clan VII* and *The Lyre*. His short story, "Zoloft," was awarded 2nd place/publication in *Into the Void* and nominated for a Pushcart Prize.

Seth Rosenbloom is a poet, performer, and management consultant. His theatrical work has appeared at On the Boards, Bumbershoot, and on the Seattle Channel. Poems have appeared or are forthcoming in *CutBank Online, Hawai'i Pacific Review, Evening Street Review*, and *The Main Street Rag*. Seth grew up in Virginia and resides in Seattle.

Eileen Rush is a queer writer, poet, and narrative designer raised in southern Appalachia and living in Louisville, Kentucky. Her work has appeared in *The Southern Review, Pleiades*, and elsewhere. She's got her a garden and abides on a farm with, depending on who you ask, too many chickens.

Susan Shaw Sailer lives in Morgantown, West Virginia, and has published three books of poetry, *The Distance Beyond Sight, The God of Roundabouts*, and *Ship of Light*, and two chapbooks, *Bulletins from a War Zone* and *COAL*. She is a member of the Madwomen in the Attic program at Carlow University.

Roberta Schultz is a singer-songwriter and poet originally from Grant's Lick, Kentucky. Three chapbooks, *Outposts on the Border of Longing* (2014), *Songs from the Shaper's Harp* (2017), and *Touchstones* (2020) were published by Finishing Line Press. Poems have appeared in *Sheila-Na-Gig, Panoply, Still: The Journal, Riparian, Kudzu, The Main Street Rag*, and others.

Randa Shannon was born in Sheffield, Alabama, came of age in Nashville, and currently lives in Pittsburgh, Pennsylvania. She is retired from nursing and urban farming. Randa participates in the Mad Women in the Attic writing program at Carlow University.

James Shipman (1953-2020) was a prominent Pittsburgh sculptor, master ceramicist, and collage artist who worked with clay, metal, wood, and found objects. In the mid-80s he began creating commissioned art pieces at his studio in the Millvale Industrial Park, later opening a studio, workshop, and exhibition gallery in the Landmarks Preservation Resource Center.

Annette Sisson has published in *Nashville Review, Typishly, One, Psaltery & Lyre*, and others. She published a chapbook with Finishing Line Press (2019), was named a 2020 BOAAT Writing Fellow, and won The Porch Writers' Collective's 2019 poetry prize. Her full-length poetry book was a finalist with Glass Lyre Press. http://annettesisson.com.

Gerald Smith, a retired professor, is the author/editor of several volumes of university history and Appalachian place studies. He spent more than a quarter century studying rural life, including farms, churches, log structures, and cemeteries. His poetry concerns the sense of loss and displacement in Appalachian settings.

Anna Egan Smucker's *No Star Nights* won the International Reading Association Children's Book Award. Two of her nine books represented West Virginia at the National Book Festival. *Fallingwater*, co-authored with Marc Harshman, was named an Amazon Children's Nonfiction Book of the Month. Her chapbook *Rowing Home* was published in 2019 by Finishing Line Press. She calls Bridgeport, WV, home. www.annasmucker.com

Sherry Cook Stanforth is the founder/director of Thomas More University's Creative Writing Vision and the Originary Arts Initiative, providing arts- and nature-inspired programming for diverse populations in the region. She is the managing editor of *Riparian: Poems, Short Prose and Photographs Inspired by the Ohio River* (Dos Madres Press, 2019), the author of *Drone String* (Bottom Dog Press, 2015), and a member of Tellico, a multi-generational family band.

Jacob Strautmann's debut book of poems, *The Land of the Dead Is Open for Business*, is available from Four Way Books. Awarded a 2018 Massachusetts Poetry Fellowship by the Massachusetts Cultural Council, his poems have appeared in *Agni, Forklift, Salamander Magazine, The Boston Globe, Appalachian Journal, Southern Humanities Review, Appalachian Heritage*, and *Quiddity*. www.jacobstrautmann.com.

Chuck Stringer is grateful to have spent another year writing with fellow regional poets in the Thomas More University Creative Writing Vision Program. His work has appeared in *For a Better World, Literary Accents, Riparian, The Licking River Review,* and *Words*. He lives with his wife, Susan, near Fowlers Fork in Union, Kentucky.

Colette Tennant is a poet and English professor who grew up in Ohio and Appalachia, now living in Oregon. She has two books of poetry, *Commotion of Wings* and *Eden and After*. Her most recent book, *Religion in The Handmaid's Tale: a Brief Guide*, was published in 2019 to coincide with Margaret Atwood's *The Testaments*.

Richard Tillinghast has published twelve books of poetry and five of creative nonfiction. His most recent publication is *Journeys into the Mind of the World: A Book of Places* (University of Tennessee Press, 2017). Poems have appeared in *The New Yorker, The Atlantic, The American Poetry Review, The Harvard Review*, and elsewhere.

Randi Ward is a poet, translator, lyricist, and photographer from West Virginia. She received the American-Scandinavian Foundation's Nadia Christensen Prize. MadHat Press published her second full-length poetry collection, *Whipstitches*, in 2016. Her work has also been featured on Folk Radio UK, NPR, and PBS NewsHour. randiward.com/about

Robb Webb (1939-2021), founding publisher of *PMS&G*, was born in Whitesburg and embraced New York City for his last 50 years. A highly successful voice artist, actor, photographer, and supporter of the arts, his photographs were exhibited in New York galleries and published in *Who Needs Parks* (Katz, Ed. Rapaport, New York, 1974), as well as this journal.

Dick Westheimer writes poetry to makes sense of the world, which is made easier by the company of his wife of 41 years and the plot of land they've worked together all that time. Poems have appeared in *Rattle, Riparian*, and *The New Verse News*, among others.

Dana Wildsmith's newest poetry collection is *One Light* (Texas Review Press, 2019). She is also the author of a novel, *Jumping*; an environmental memoir, *Back to Abnormal: Surviving with an Old Farm in the New South*, a finalist for Georgia Author of the Year; and five collections of poetry. She is a Fellow of the Hambidge Center for Creative Arts and Sciences.

Mike Wilson's work has appeared in *Appalachian Heritage, Solidago, Fiction Southeast, Deep South Magazine,* and *Anthology of Appalachian Writers Vol. X,* among others. He is author of *Arranging Deck Chairs on the Titanic* (Rabbit House Press, 2020) and resides in central Kentucky. mikewilsonwriter.com

Amy Wright's nonfiction debut, *Paper Concert: A Conversation in the Round,* is published by Sarabande Books. The author of three poetry books, essays have appeared in *The Georgia Review, Fourth Genre, Ninth Letter, Brevity,* and elsewhere. Originally from a family farm in southwest Virginia, she was awarded two Peter Taylor Fellowships to the Kenyon Review Writers Workshop, among other honors.

After Vietnam, Uncle Sam aided **Jack Wright** with his newly acquired nonfunctioning inner spirits. Recently, as an old man, he decided to carve personal life stories to help rid himself of ancient cobwebs that hindered his glaucomic vision of pink flamingoes and Jim Webb. He was last spotted in cheeky Athens, Ohio.

Submission Guidelines
Volume 25:
Appalachia (Un)Masked

Deadline: April 15, 2022
Response: Late June, 2022
Publication Date: October 2022

What or who shall be revealed? How can we come to know what lurks behind the veil—or behind the walls, intentions, closed doors, uniforms, costumes, logos, packaging, blinders, and fig leaves of our own making? In creative variety, we mask (or unmask) our bodies, behaviors, and agendas. Masquerades leave us guessing over phantoms as well as Shakespearean lovers. In gothic spirit, crazed characters cover up crimes, tucking bodies beneath floorboards...inside catacombs...down wells...into a river's swift current. Sometimes, heroes show up to dig for the truth.

Born of two formerly enslaved Kentuckians, Paul Laurence Dunbar complicates interpretations of human guile, where some are forced to "wear the mask that grins and lies" in order to survive the dangerous maze of American democracy. Plato's ancient (and ironic) wisdom suggests that "those who are able to see beyond the shadows and lies of their culture will never be understood" or believed by the public. One lie (or 30,500-plus lies) may crumble a community. *What will happen* if we cover—or don't cover—our faces during a pandemic? Prophets preach their warnings: "But there is nothing…hidden that will not be known. Accordingly, whatever you have said in the dark shall be heard in the light…" (Luke 12:2-3).

Nature, too, echoes our masking dilemmas. Liar's moon or high noon? Downy woodpeckers hammer away at trees, camouflaged. Ovenbirds play wounded and possums play dead to disguise their vulnerability. Raccoons boldly pose as bandits of our bounty, while snakes, crawdads and salamanders tuck themselves under creek stones, unseen. Redbuds and ridges refuse to blend in—they stand out memorably until they are uprooted. Blankets of snow, killing frost, water's lacy veil, a cloak of fog, the peel-away parchment of sycamores and birches. Our own nature leads us into the bunkers and bubbles and caves of time. There, we must choose to fight or flee. To see or not to see. Be seen—or hide away.

***

Drawing on the spirit of Appalachia, how will you reveal the masked or unmasked facets of a past, present, or future time? For Volume 25, we are asking for your poems, short stories, essays, flash pieces and black and white 2D art in response to the theme, *Appalachia (Un)Masked*. We mostly accept unpublished work, but we aren't sticklers.

We are are pleased to consider unsolicited reviews of recent books by Appalachian writers, especially those whose work has appeared in *PMS&G*, regardless of whether the books reviewed fit the particular theme. We also solicit reviews

for a few new books we would like to feature in the journal
(See **New Books**).

Full guidelines can be found here: http://www.sawconline.
net/pmsg-submission-guidelines.html
or emailed upon request to pmsg.journal@gmail.com.

PLEASE, PLEASE, PLEASE follow these guidelines
if you would like for us to consider your submission.
Work pasted directly into the email message or sent as
PDF attachment, or in other fonts or formatting is time-
consuming to reformat and makes us cranky, as does
opening up a bunch of documents from the same person,
or having to trace unlabeled pieces back to their author's
email. And you don't want cranky editors, now, do you?